Twenty-Four Unusual Stories For Boys And Girls

Anna Cogswell Tyler

Twenty-Four Unusual Stories For Boys And Girls
THE CONVENT FREE FROM CARE

ONCE when the Emperor Charles V was traveling in the country, he saw a convent, and in passing by a little door he read this strange inscription:

"Here you live without a care."

The Emperor was very surprised and could scarcely believe his eyes.

"It seems to me an impossibility," he thought; "does some one really exist on earth who is free from care? As Emperor I am overwhelmed with troubles, while here in this convent, which is a little kingdom in itself, one would have nothing to worry about. I cannot believe it."

Immediately on setting foot in the village inn, the Emperor sent the hostess to fetch the Abbot of this singular convent.

You can imagine what a state of mind the latter was in when he heard he was summoned to the Emperor's presence.

"What have I done to displease him?" he asked himself. On the way he examined his conscience over and over again, and he could think of no fault of which he was guilty. "I am in troubled waters; I must steer my way through," he said.

When he was in the Emperor's presence, the latter expressed his astonishment of what he had read.

The Abbot now knew why he had been summoned, and smiled. "Sir," said he, "does that astonish you? However, it is very simple; we eat, we drink, we sleep, and worry over nothing."

"Well, Reverend Abbot, that state of things must come to an end," said the Emperor, "and in order that you may have your share of trouble, I command you to bring me to-morrow the answers to the three following questions:

"First, What is the depth of the sea?

"Secondly, How many cows' tails would it take to measure the distance between the earth and the sun?

"Thirdly, What am I thinking about?

"Try to please me or I shall exact a penalty from you."

On hearing these words, the Abbot returned to his convent with a heavy heart. From that moment he knew no peace. He cudgeled his brains as to what answer he could make to the Emperor.

When the little bell of the abbey rang, summoning the monks to prayer in the chapel, the Abbot continued to pace his garden. He was so deep in thought that he was quite oblivious of what was taking place around him. Even if a thunderbolt had fallen at his feet, he would not have noticed it.

"What a horrible thing," he thought. "Is it possible that such a misfortune has overtaken me? I cannot possibly answer. Who can save the situation? Perhaps our shepherd could; he has a very lively imagination; but talk of the devil—"

At that identical moment the shepherd appeared, leading his flock. He was very surprised to see the Abbot, who was always without a care, mediating in solitude.

What could have happened?

Without more ado he went to him, and asked him what was troubling him so deeply.

"Yes, I deserve to be pitied," said the Abbot, and he told him what had happened.

"Why are you tormenting yourself over a little thing like that?" the shepherd laughingly replied. "Leave it to me, and all will be well. To-morrow I will come here and dress myself in your robe, and I will turn the tables on him."

At first the Abbot demurred, but in the end he yielded, and the matter was settled.

The next day the shepherd went boldly to find the Emperor.

"Well, Reverend Abbot," the Emperor said with serenity, "have you found out the answers?"

3

"Yes, certainly, sire."

"Speak, I am listening."

"Sire, the sea is as deep as a stone's throw.

"To measure the distance between the earth and the sun, you only need one cow's tail, if it is long enough.

"Do you wish to know, sire, what you are thinking? Well, at this moment, you think, sire, that the Abbot of the convent is in your presence, and it is only his shepherd."

The Emperor laughed so heartily that if he has not stopped laughing he is laughing still.

"WHAT THE GOOD-MAN DOES IS SURE TO BE RIGHT!"

I AM going to tell you a story that was told to me when I was a little one, and which I like better and better the oftener I think of it. For it is with stories as with some men and women, the older they grow, the pleasanter they grow, and that is delightful!

Of course you have been into the country? Well, then, you must have seen a regularly poor old cottage. Moss and weeds spring up amid the thatch of the roof, a stork's nest decorates the chimney (the stork can never be dispensed with), the walls are aslant, the windows low (in fact, only one of them can be shut), the baking-oven projects forward, and an elder-bush leans over the gate, where you will see a tiny pond with a duck and ducklings in it, close under a knotted old willow-tree. Yes, and then there is a watch-dog that barks at every passer-by.

Just such a poor little cottage as this was the one in my story, and in it dwelt a husband and wife. Few as their possessions were, one of them they could do without, and that was a horse, that used to graze in the ditch beside the highroad. The good-man rode on it to town, he lent it to his neighbors, and received slight services from them in return, but still it would be more profitable to sell the horse, or else exchange it for something they could make of more frequent use. But which should they do? sell, or exchange?

"Why, you will find out what is best, good-man," said the wife. "Isn't this market-day? Come, ride off to the town—get money, or what you can for the horse—whatever you do is sure to be right. Make haste for the market!"

So she tied on his neckerchief—for that was a matter she understood better than he—she tied it with a double knot, and made him look quite spruce; she dusted his hat with the palm of her hand; and she kissed him and sent him off, riding the horse that was to be either sold or bartered. Of course, he would know what to do.

The sun was hot, and not a cloud in the sky. The road was dusty, and such a crowd of folk passed on their way to market. Some in wagons, some on horseback, some on their own legs. A fierce sun and no shade all the way.

5

A man came driving a cow — as pretty a cow as could be. "That creature must give beautiful milk," thought the peasant; "it would not be a bad bargain if I got that. I say, you fellow with the cow!" he began aloud: "let's have some talk together. Look you, a horse, I believe, costs more than a cow, but it is all the same to me, as I have more use for a cow — shall we make an exchange?"

"To be sure!" was the answer, and the bargain was made.

The good-man might just as well now turn back homeward — he had finished his business. But he had made up his mind to go to market, so to market he must go, if only to look on, so, with his cow, he continued on his way. He trudged fast, so did the cow, and soon they overtook a man who was leading a sheep — a sheep in good condition, well clothed with wool.

"I should very much like to have that!" said the peasant. "It would find pasture enough by our road-side, and in winter we might take it into our own room. And really it would be more reasonable for us to be keeping a sheep than a cow. Shall we exchange?"

Yes, the man who owned the sheep was quite willing; so the exchange was made, and the good-man now went on with his sheep. Presently there passed him a man with a big goose under his arm.

"Well, you have got a heavy fellow there!" quoth the peasant. "Feathers and fat in plenty! How nicely we could tie her up near our little pond, and it would be something for the good-wife to gather up the scraps for. She has often said: 'If we had but a goose!' Now she can have one — and she shall, too! Will you exchange? I will give you my sheep for your goose, and say 'thank you' besides."

The other had no objection, so the peasant had his will and his goose. He was now close to the town; he was wearied with the heat and the crowd, folk and cattle pushing past him, thronging on the road, in the ditch, and close up to the turnpike-man's cabbage-garden, where his one hen was tied up, lest in her fright she should lose her way and be carried off. It was a short-backed hen: she winked with one eye, crying, "Cluck, cluck!" What she was thinking of I can't say, but what the peasant thought on seeing her, was this: "That is the prettiest hen I have ever seen—much prettier than any of our parson's chickens. I should very much like to have her. A hen can always pick up a grain here and there—can provide for herself. I almost think it would be a good plan to take her instead of the goose. Shall we exchange?" he asked. "Exchange?" repeated the owner; "not a bad idea!" So it was done; the turnpike-man got the goose, the peasant the hen.

He had transacted a deal of business since first starting on his way to the town; hot was he, and wearied too; he must have a dram and a bit of bread. He was on the point of entering an inn, when the innkeeper met him in the doorway swinging a sack chock-full of something.

"What have you there?" asked the peasant.

"Mellow apples," was the answer, "a whole sackful for swine."

"What a quantity! wouldn't my wife like to see so many! Why, the last year we had only one single apple on the whole tree at home. Ah! I wish my wife could see them!"

"Well, what will you give me for them?"

"Give for them? why, I will give you my hen." So he gave the hen, took the apples, and entered the inn, and going straight up to the bar, set his sack upright against the stove without considering that there was a fire lighted inside. A good many strangers were present, among them two Englishmen, both with their pockets full of gold, and fond of laying wagers, as Englishmen in stories are wont to be.

Presently there came a sound from the stove, "Suss—suss—suss!" the apples were roasting. "What is that?" folk asked, and soon heard the whole history of the horse that had been exchanged, first for a cow, and lastly for a sack of rotten apples.

"Well! won't you get a good sound cuff from your wife, when you go home?" said one of the Englishmen. "Something heavy enough to fell an ox, I warn you!"

"I shall get kisses, not cuffs," replied the peasant. "My wife will say, 'Whatever the good-man does is right.'"

"A wager!" cried the Englishmen, "for a hundred pounds?"

"Say rather a bushelful," quoth the peasant, "and I can only lay my bushel of apples with myself and the good-wife, but that will be more than full measure, I trow."

"Done!" cried they. And the innkeeper's cart was brought out forthwith, the Englishmen got into it, the peasant got into it, the rotten apples got into it, and away they sped to the peasant's cottage.

"Good evening, wife."

"Same to you, good-man."

"Well, I have exchanged the horse, not sold it."

"Of course," said the wife, taking his hand, and in her eagerness to listen noticing neither the sack nor the strangers.

"I exchanged the horse for a cow."

"O! how delightful! now we can have milk, butter, and cheese, on our table. What a capital idea!"

"Yes, but I exchanged the cow for a sheep."

"Better and better!" cried the wife. "You are always so thoughtful; we have only just grass enough for a sheep. But now we shall have ewe's milk, and ewe's cheese, and woolen stockings, nay, woolen jackets too; and a cow would not give us that; she loses all her hairs. But you are always such a clever fellow."

"But the ewe I exchanged again for a goose."

"What! shall we really keep Michaelmas this year, good-man? You are always thinking of what will please me, and that was a beautiful thought. The goose can be tethered to the willow-tree and grow fat for Michaelmas Day."

"But I gave the goose away for a hen," said the peasant.

"A hen? well, that was a good exchange," said his wife. "A hen will lay eggs, sit upon them, and we shall have chickens. Fancy! a hen-yard! that is just the thing I have always wished for most."

8

"Ah, but I exchanged the hen for a sack of mellow apples."

"Then I must give thee a kiss," cried the wife. "Thanks, my own husband. And now I have something to tell. When you were gone I thought how I could get a right good dinner ready for you: omelets with parsley. Now I had the eggs, but not the parsley. So I went over to the schoolmaster's; they have parsley, I know, but the woman is so crabbed, she wanted something for it. Now what could I give her? nothing grows in our garden, not even a rotten apple, not even that had I for her; but now I can give her ten, nay, a whole sackful. That is famous, good-man!" and she kissed him again.

"Well done!" cried the Englishmen. "Always down hill, and always happy! Such a sight is worth the money!" And so quite contentedly they paid the bushelful of gold pieces to the peasant, who had got kisses, not cuffs, by his bargains.

Certainly virtue is her own reward, when the wife is sure that her husband is the wisest man in the world, and that whatever he does is right. So now you have heard this old story that was once told to me, and I hope have learnt the moral.

WHERE TO LAY THE BLAME

Many and many a man has come to trouble — so he will say — by following his wife's advice. This is how it was with a man of whom I shall tell you.

THERE was once upon a time a fisherman who had fished all day long and had caught not so much as a sprat. So at night there he sat by the fire, rubbing his knees and warming his shins, and waiting for supper that his wife was cooking for him, and his hunger was as sharp as vinegar, and his temper hot enough to fry fat.

While he sat there grumbling and growling and trying to make himself comfortable and warm, there suddenly came a knock at the door. The good woman opened it, and there stood an old man, clad all in red from head to foot, and with a snowy beard at his chin as white as winter snow.

The fisherman's wife stood gasping and staring at the strange figure, but the old man in red walked straight into the hut. "Bring your nets, fisherman," said he, "and come with me. There is something that I want you to catch for me, and if I have luck I will pay you for your fishing as never fisherman was paid before."

"Not I," said the fisherman; "I go out no more this night. I have been fishing all day long until my back is nearly broken, and have caught nothing, and now I am not such a fool as to go out and leave a good supper and a warm fire at your bidding." But the fisherman's wife had listened to what the old man had said about paying for the job, and she was of a different mind from her husband. "Come," said she, "the old man promises to pay you well. This is not a chance to be lost, I can tell you, and my advice to you is that you go."

The fisherman shook his head. No, he would not go; he had said he would not, and he would not. But the wife only smiled and said again, "My advice to you is that you go."

The fisherman grumbled and grumbled, and swore that he would not go. The wife said nothing but one thing. She did not argue; she did not lose her temper; she only said to everything that he said, "My advice to you is that you go."

At last the fisherman's anger boiled over. "Very well," said he, spitting his words at her; "if you drive me out into the night, I suppose I will have to go." And then he spoke the words that so many men say: "Many a man has come to trouble by following his wife's advice."

Then down he took his fur cap and up he took his nets, and off he and the old man marched through the moonlight, their shadows bobbing along like black spiders behind them.

Well, on they went, out from the town and across the fields and through the woods, until at last they came to a dreary, lonesome desert, where nothing was to be seen but gray rocks and weeds and thistles.

"Well," said the fisherman, "I have fished, man and boy, for forty-seven years, but never did I see as unlikely a place to catch anything as this."

But the old man said never a word. First of all he drew a great circle with strange figures, marking it with his finger upon the ground. Then out from under his red gown he brought a tinder-box and steel, and a little silver casket covered all over with strange figures of serpents and dragons and what not. He brought some sticks of spice-wood from his pouch, and then he struck a light and made a fire. Out of the box he took a gray powder, which he flung upon the little blaze.

Puff! flash! A vivid flame went up into the moonlight, and then a dense smoke as black as ink, which spread out wider and wider, far and near, till all below was darker than the darkest midnight. Then the old man began to utter strange spells and words.

Presently there began a rumbling that sounded louder and louder and nearer and nearer, until it roared and bellowed like thunder. The earth rocked and swayed, and the poor fisherman shook and trembled with fear till his teeth chattered in his head.

Then suddenly the roaring and bellowing ceased, and all was as still as death, though the darkness was as thick and black as ever. "Now," said the old magician—for such he was—"now we are about to take a journey such as no one ever traveled before. Heed well what I tell you. Speak not a single word, for if you do, misfortune will be sure to happen."

"Ain't I to say anything?" said the fisherman.

"No."

"Not even 'boo' to a goose?"

"No."

"Well, that is pretty hard upon a man who likes to say his say," said the fisherman.

"And moreover," said the old man, "I must blindfold you as well." Thereupon he took from his pocket a handkerchief, and made ready to tie it about the fisherman's eyes.

"And ain't I to see anything at all?" said the fisherman.

"No."

"Not even so much as a single feather?"

"No."

"Well, then," said the fisherman, "I wish I'd not come."

But the old man tied the handkerchief tightly around his eyes, and then he was as blind as a bat.

"Now," said the old man, "throw your leg over what you feel and hold fast."

The fisherman reached down his hand, and there felt the back of something rough and hairy. He flung his leg over it, and whisk! whizz! off he shot through the air like a sky-rocket. Nothing was left for him to do but grip tightly with hands and feet and to hold fast. On they went, and on they went, until, after a great while, whatever it was that was carrying him lit upon the ground, and there the fisherman found himself standing, for that which had brought him had gone.

The old man whipped the handkerchief off his eyes, and there the fisherman found himself on the shores of the sea, where there was nothing to be seen but water upon one side and rocks and naked sand upon the other.

"This is the place for you to cast your nets," said the old magician; "for if we catch nothing here we catch nothing at all."

The fisherman unrolled his nets and cast them and dragged them, and then cast them and dragged them again, but neither time caught so much as a herring. But the third time that he cast he found that he had caught something that weighed as heavy as lead. He pulled and pulled, until by-and-by he dragged the load ashore, and what should it be but a great chest of wood, blackened by sea-water, and covered with shells and green moss.

That was the very thing that the magician had come to fish for. From his pouch the old man took a little golden key, which he fitted into a key-hole in the side of the chest. He threw back the lid; the fisherman looked within, and there was the prettiest little palace that man's eye ever beheld, all made of mother-of-pearl and silver-frosted as white as snow. The old magician lifted the little palace out of the box and set it upon the ground.

Then, lo and behold! a marvelous thing happened; for the palace instantly began to grow for all the world like a soap-bubble, until it stood in the moonlight gleaming and glistening like snow, the windows bright with the lights of a thousand wax tapers, and the sound of music and voices and laughter coming from within.

Hardly could the fisherman catch his breath from one strange thing when another happened. The old magician took off his clothes and his face — yes, his face — for all the world as though it had been a mask, and there stood as handsome and noble a young man as ever the light looked on. Then, beckoning to the fisherman, dumb with wonder, he led the way up the great flight of marble steps to the palace door. As he came the door swung open with a blaze of light, and there stood hundreds of noblemen, all clad in silks and satins and velvets, who, when they saw the magician, bowed low before him, as though he had been a king. Leading the way, they brought the two through halls and chambers and room after room, each more magnificent than the other, until they came to one that surpassed a hundredfold any of the others.

At the farther end was a golden throne, and upon it sat a lady more lovely and beautiful than a dream, her eyes as bright as diamonds, her cheeks like rose leaves, and her hair like spun gold. She came half-way down the steps of the throne to welcome the magician, and when the two met they kissed one another before all those who were looking on. Then she brought him to the throne and seated him beside her, and there they talked for a long time very earnestly.

Nobody said a word to the fisherman, who stood staring about him like an owl. "I wonder," said he to himself at last, "if they will give a body a bite to eat by-and-by?" for, to tell the truth, the good supper he had come away from at home had left a sharp hunger gnawing at his insides, and he longed for something good and warm to fill the empty place. But time passed, and not so much as a crust of bread was brought to stay his stomach.

By-and-by the clock struck twelve, and then the two who sat upon the throne arose. The beautiful lady took the magician by the hand, and, turning to those who stood around, said, in a loud voice, "Behold him who alone is worthy to possess the jewel of jewels! Unto him do I give it, and with it all power of powers!" Thereon she opened a golden casket that stood beside her, and brought thence a little crystal ball, about as big as a pigeon's egg, in which was something that glistened like a spark of fire. The magician took the crystal ball and thrust it into his bosom; but what it was the fisherman could not guess, and if you do not know I shall not tell you.

Then for the first time the beautiful lady seemed to notice the fisherman. She beckoned him, and when he stood beside her two men came carrying a chest. The chief treasurer opened it, and it was full of bags of gold money. "How will you have it?" said the beautiful lady.

"Have what?" said the fisherman.

"Have the pay for your labor?" said the beautiful lady.

"I will," said the fisherman, promptly, "take it in my hat."

"So be it," said the beautiful lady. She waved her hand, and the chief treasurer took a bag from the chest, untied it, and emptied a cataract of gold into the fur cap. The fisherman had never seen so much wealth in all his life before, and he stood like a man turned to stone.

"Is all this mine?" said the fisherman.

"It is," said the beautiful lady.

"Then God bless your pretty eyes," said the fisherman.

Then the magician kissed the beautiful lady, and, beckoning to the fisherman, left the throne room the same way that they had come. The noblemen, in silks and satins and velvets, marched ahead, and back they went through the other apartments, until at last they came to the door. Out they stepped, and then what do you suppose happened!

If the wonderful palace had grown like a bubble, like a bubble it vanished. There the two stood on the sea-shore, with nothing to be seen but rocks and sand and water, and the starry sky overhead. The fisherman shook his cap of gold, and it jingled and tinkled, and was as heavy as lead. If it was not all a dream, he was rich for life. "But anyhow," said he, "they might have given a body a bite to eat."

The magician put on his red clothes and his face again, making himself as hoary and as old as before. He took out flint and steel, and his sticks of spice-wood and his gray powder, and made a great fire and smoke just as he had done before. Then again he tied his handkerchief over the fisherman's eyes. "Remember," said he, "what I told you when we started upon our journey. Keep your mouth tight shut, for if you utter so much as a single word you are a lost man. Now throw your leg over what you feel and hold fast."

The fisherman had his net over one arm and his cap of gold in the other hand; nevertheless, there he felt the same hairy thing he had felt before. He flung his leg over it, and away he was gone through the air like a sky-rocket.

Now, he had grown somewhat used to strange things by this time, so he began to think he would like to see what sort of a creature it was upon which he was riding thus through the sky. So he contrived, in spite of his net and cap, to push up the handkerchief from over one eye. Out he peeped, and then he saw what the strange steed was. He was riding upon a he-goat as black as night, and in front of him was the magician riding upon just such another, his great red robe fluttering out in the moonlight like huge red wings.

"Great herring and little fishes!" roared the fisherman; "it is a billy-goat!"

Instantly goats, old man, and all were gone like a flash. Down fell the fisherman through the empty sky, whirling over and over and around and around like a frog. He held tightly to his net, but away flew his fur cap, the golden money falling in a shower like sparks of yellow light. Down he fell and down he fell, until his head spun like a top.

By good-luck his house was just below, with its thatch of soft rushes. Into the very middle of it he tumbled, and right through the thatch — bump! — into the room below.

The good wife was in bed, snoring away for dear life; but such a noise as the fisherman made coming into the house was enough to wake the dead. Up she jumped, and there she sat, staring and winking with sleep, and with her brains as addled as a duck's egg in a thunderstorm.

"There!" said the fisherman, as he gathered himself up and rubbed his shoulder, "that is what comes of following a woman's advice!"

THE WINDS, THE BIRDS, AND THE TELEGRAPH WIRES

LONG, long ago, a hundred times as long as any one can remember, the Great Earth King became so very, very busy about a great many things that there were several things that he could not do. So he sat himself down and rested his great head upon his hand, and thought, and thought, and thought until he decided that he must have some assistance. He would advertise for some messengers! So he seized a great brush, as big as a church steeple, dipped it into the red and golden sunset light, and wrote in big letters high on the sky, that every one far and near could read:

WANTED! MESSENGERS! FLEETER THAN HORSES, SWIFTER THAN MEN, TO CARRY MY MESSAGES, A MILLION TIMES TEN.

and he signed it simply, "The Earth King." Then he went into his rainbow house and laid himself down to sleep on his rainbow bed.

He had scarcely fallen asleep when there came a rustle, rustle, rustle at the rainbow window, and a rattle, rattle, rattle at the rainbow door. He sprang quickly from his great bed.

"Who be ye?" he asked.

"We be messengers," came the reply, "come to serve the King."

Then the King opened the door. There before him stood four of the strangest creatures that he had ever seen. They were so light that they could stand on nothing; they had great wide wings; they had pale faces and gleaming eyes; and they had light garments that floated and flapped and fluttered in the breeze.

"What are your names?" asked the King.

"We are the Winds," answered the mightiest of the four, "East Wind, West Wind, South Wind, North Wind," pointing to each in turn, himself last. "We have come—

Fleeter than horses, swifter than men,

To carry your messages, a million times ten."

Then the King spoke to them in deep and solemn tone: "The task is a great one. The King's business is grave and important. My messengers must be swift and faithful. Are ye able?"

Then the four winds piously crossed their breasts with their wings and whispered, "Try us and see, try us and see, try us and see."

So the King tried them.

"Down by the sea," said the King, "far over the mountains, many hours away, there lives a fisher folk that I love. Every day the men of the village go forth in their little boats to fish, and every evening they come home with their catch. But of late thick and heavy clouds have hung about them. They have not dared go forth lest they should not reach home again, and their families begin to be in want. Go to them to-day. Drive away the fog and clouds that the people may be happy again. Quick! away!"

Then the four winds lifted their swift, beautiful wings and were gone. Faster and faster they flew till none could tell how fast they flew. Over the meadows they went and over the mountains. Each tried to outwing the others until it became a fierce and careless game. So blind and careless were they in their sport that they did not notice how they whirled the sand, and broke the trees, and tossed the water. Swiftly through the fishing village they tore, hurling its poor houses to the ground and crashing, dashing, slashing, smashing the waves upon the fallen wrecks and the frightened and suffering folk.

Not until they were weary with their furious sport did they remember the errand on which the King had sent them. They retraced their steps as quickly as they could, but alas! to their shame and grief, the village lay in ruins and the people wept for their loss.

Then the Earth King was very sad and angry. He brought the shameful winds before his court. "False and faithless winds," he said, in stern and awful voice, "ye did not do my errand; ye were traitors to your trust; great shall be your punishment. Nevermore shall ye be my messengers, evermore shall ye be my slaves. Away from my sight!"

Then the faithless winds departed from before the face of the King, and in shame and sorrow went moaning among the caves and the rocks by the seaside, and sighing among the lonely pine trees in the wilderness, and even to this day you may hear the echoes of their moans and sighs.

The Earth King was sorrowful, but not discouraged. Again he seized the great paint brush, as big as a church steeple, dipped it into the red and golden sunset light, and wrote in big letters high on the sky that every one far and near could read:

WANTED! MESSENGERS!

FLEETER THAN HORSES,

SWIFTER THAN MEN,

TO CARRY MY MESSAGES,

A MILLION TIMES TEN.

Then he went into his rainbow house and laid himself down on his rainbow bed. He scarcely had taken forty winks when he heard a rat-tat-tatting on the rainbow window and a rap-rap-rapping on the rainbow door. Quickly he leaped from his great bed.

"Who be ye?" he asked.

"We be messengers," came a gentle voice through the keyhole, "come to serve the King."

Then he opened the door, and there before him flitted and twittered a company of the most curious little people that he ever had set eyes upon. They had each a pair of beady eyes, a little pointed nose, a set of little scratchy toes, and the softest kind of a coat, fitting as snug as ever the tailor could make it.

"What are your names?" asked the King.

"We are the birds, and our names are many. We saw the King's sign in the sky and have come—

Fleeter than horses, swifter than men,

To carry your messages, a million times ten."

Then the King, remembering the Winds, addressed them in very deep and solemn tones: "The task is a great one. The King's business is exceeding grave and important. My messengers must be swift and faithful, must remember my commands and keep my secrets. Are ye able?"

Each bird laid his little scratchy toes on his little pointed nose and vowed that he would remember the King's commands and keep the King's secrets.

"Then," said the King, "make ready. Far to the north dwells a people that I love. For many a month they have lived amid ice and snow and the bitter frosts. Now they sigh for warmer days, and I have heard them. I am planning a delightful surprise for them. I am going to carry spring to them. Go, find the warm sunshine and the soft south wind and bid them come at once to the King's court, that I may take them and the spring days to my suffering and discouraged people. Then return with all speed to the King, and remember — do not betray my secret."

The bird-messengers hastened away as fast as ever their wings could carry them. They summoned the warm sunshine and the soft south wind and bade them make haste to the Earth King. They, of course, turned back as they were commanded, but before they reached home again, each one of them was seized with a strange, restless, uneasy feeling right in the middle of his feathers. It must have been the secret trying to get out. One by one they stole past the King's house under cover of the night and made their way to the north country. And when the morning came, there they were, sitting on the fence posts and in the apple trees, just bursting with the happy secret of the King.

Then the robin pipped, and the bluebird blew;

The sparrow chipped, and the swallow, too:

"We know something, — we won't tell, —

Somebody's coming, — you know well.

This is his name ('twixt you and me),

S-P-R-I-N-G."

The people were very happy when they heard what the birds said, and with much excitement began to get ready for the springtime.

Now, of course, the King knew nothing about all this, and was very happy in thinking of the surprise that he was to give the people. He took the warm sunshine and the soft south wind for companions, and made his way in all haste to the land of ice and snow. As he arrived, with his delightful secret, as he thought, hidden in his heart, he was amazed to find an old woman sitting in her doorway knitting.

"Why are you sitting here?" he asked. "Why are you not within, warming your feet by the fire?"

"Why, don't you know?" she said, "spring is coming!"

"Spring?" he asked, almost roughly; "how do you know?"

"Oh," said she with a smile, trying not to look at a robin that turned his back behind the picket fence, hoping that if the King saw him he might think he was an English sparrow, "a little bird told me."

The King walked up the street, looking gloomy enough, and soon came across a gardener with his rake, uncovering the crocuses and the daffodils.

"Why do you do this, my good man? Surely your flowers will freeze. You had much better be covering them up."

"Oh, no," he said, straightening his bent back, "spring is coming."

"Spring," said the King; "how do you know?"

"Oh," said the gardener, with a grin, and a twinkle in his left eye, as he caught sight of a bluebird peeking half-scared around the limb of a near-by apple tree, "a little bird told me."

Then the disgraceful story all came out: that

The robin pipped, and the bluebird blew;

The sparrow chipped, and the swallow, too:

"We know something, — we won't tell, —

Somebody's coming, — you know well.

This is his name ('twixt you and me),

S-P-R-I-N-G."

My! but wasn't the Earth King disgusted! And weren't the bird-messengers ashamed to come when he sternly called them! Each laid his little pointed nose on his little scratchy toes, and dropped his eyes and uttered never a word.

"Silly birds," he said in scornful voice. "You vowed to keep my secrets. You have broken your vow. You obeyed my commands and called the south wind and the sunshine; so I cannot be too harsh with you. But you cannot keep my secrets, so I cannot keep you as my messengers. Now and then I may use you as my servants. Adieu!"

Then the birds flew sadly away as quietly and quickly as ever they could, and set to work building their nests in holes in the trees and holes in the ground and in out-of-the-way places, making such a chattering meantime that neither they, nor any one else, could hear themselves think.

By this time the Earth King was nearly discouraged. He did not know what in the world to do. He rested his elbow on his knee and his great head in his hand and thought and wondered. Then once again he rose and took the great brush and wrote the same big words on the sky. And for very weariness he lay down on a great bank of clouds and soon was sound asleep. As he slept, the cloud grew bigger and bigger and blacker and blacker, and the thunder came nearer and nearer until, all at once, CRASH-CRASH—the cloud seemed torn to pieces and the King leaped to his feet half-scared to death, even if he was a King. There before him, darting this way and that way, and up and down, and across-ways, was a swarm of little red-hot creatures that hissed and buzzed and cracked like the Fourth of July.

"Who are you?" he asked in half-fright as he rubbed his eyes, "and what do you want?"

"Messengers, messengers, messengers," whispered they all at once, "and we have come to serve the King."

"What are your names?"

"We are the Lightning Spirits; sometimes men call us Electricity —

The swiftest creatures that are known to men,

To carry your messages, a million times ten."

The King charged them gravely and solemnly, as he had done the winds and the birds before them, that his messengers must be true and faithful and must keep his secrets. But no matter how great the task nor how heavy the oaths with which he bound them to be faithful, they were eager, all of them, to serve the King. Only he must build road-ways for them. They had not wings to fly, and their feet were not accustomed to the highways of the land. They might lose their way. So the King decided to try them. He called his laborers and ordered them to erect tall poles, and from pole to pole to lay slender roadways of wire. Miles and miles of these roadways he built, over the hills and through the valleys. And when all was complete, he called the spirits to him and whispered to them his secret messages. Quick as thought they ran over the little roadways, hither and thither, and back again, doing faithfully and well the King's errands and keeping the King's secrets. They whispered never so much as a word of them. So the Earth King called a great assembly, and before them all appointed the Lightning Spirits to be his trusted messengers for ever and a day.

Of course the winds were very jealous when they heard of it, and they determined to get revenge by stealing the messages from the spirits. They dashed against the wires day after day, trying to break them and get the secrets, but all to no purpose. All they could hear was MUM-MUM-MUM-M-M; and the harder they blew, the louder they heard it.

The birds had all along been sorry that they had given away the great secret, and had been hoping that the King would give them another chance. They were much too gentle to do as the winds did. But they were very curious to find out what the King's messages were. So day after day they went to the wires and sat upon them and snuggled down as close to them as they could get and listened hard, putting now the right ear down and now the left—but all they could ever hear was MUM-MUM-MUM-M-M-M-M.

And they seem never to have got over that habit! If you want to find out for yourself the truth of this tale, you go some day when the wind is blowing against the wires and the birds are sitting upon them, snuggled close, and put your ear to a telegraph pole and all youwill hear is MUM-MUM-MUM-M-M-M.

KATCHA AND THE DEVIL
THE STORY OF A CLINGING VINE

THERE was once a woman named Katcha who lived in a village where she owned her own cottage and garden. She had money besides but little good it did her because she was such an ill-tempered vixen that nobody, not even the poorest laborer, would marry her. Nobody would even work for her, no matter what she paid, for she couldn't open her mouth without scolding, and whenever she scolded she raised her shrill voice until you could hear it a mile away. The older she grew the worse she became until by the time she was forty she was as sour as vinegar.

Now as it always happens in a village, every Sunday afternoon there was a dance either at the burgomaster's, or at the tavern. As soon as the bagpipes sounded, the boys all crowded into the room and the girls gathered outside and looked in the windows. Katcha was always the first at the window. The music would strike up and the boys would beckon the girls to come in and dance, but no one ever beckoned Katcha. Even when she paid the piper no one ever asked her to dance. Yet she came Sunday after Sunday just the same.

One Sunday afternoon as she was hurrying to the tavern she thought to herself: "Here I am getting old and yet I've never once danced with a boy! Plague take it, to-day I'd dance with the devil if he asked me!"

She was in a fine rage by the time she reached the tavern, where she sat down near the stove and looked around to see what girls the boys had invited to dance.

Suddenly a stranger in hunter's green came in. He sat down at a table near Katcha and ordered drink. When the serving maid brought the beer, he reached over to Katcha and asked her to drink with him. At first she was much taken back at this attention, then she pursed her lips coyly and pretended to refuse, but finally she accepted.

When they had finished drinking, he pulled a ducat from his pocket, tossed it to the piper, and called out:

"Clear the floor, boys! This is for Katcha and me alone!"

25

The boys snickered and the girls giggled, hiding behind each other and stuffing their aprons into their mouths so that Katcha wouldn't hear them laughing. But Katcha wasn't noticing them at all. Katcha was dancing with a fine young man! If the whole world had been laughing at her, Katcha wouldn't have cared.

The stranger danced with Katcha all afternoon and all evening. Not once did he dance with any one else. He bought her marzipan and sweet drinks and, when the hour came to go home, he escorted her through the village.

"Ah," sighed Katcha when they reached her cottage and it was time to part, "I wish I could dance with you forever!"

"Very well," said the stranger. "Come with me."

"Where do you live?"

"Put your arm around my neck and I'll tell you."

Katcha put both arms about his neck and instantly the man changed into a devil and flew straight down to hell.

At the gates of hell he stopped and knocked.

His comrades came and opened the gates and when they saw that he was exhausted, they tried to take Katcha off his neck. But Katcha held on tight and nothing they could do or say would make her budge.

The devil finally had to appear before the Prince of Darkness himself with Katcha still glued to his neck.

"What's that thing you've got around your neck?" the Prince asked.

So the devil told how as he was walking about on earth he had heard Katcha say she would dance with the devil himself if he asked her. "So I asked her to dance with me," the devil said. "Afterwards just to frighten her a little I brought her down to hell. And now she won't let go of me!"

"Serve you right, you dunce!" the Prince said. "How often have I told you to use common sense when you go wandering around on earth! You might have known Katcha would never let go of a man once she had him!"

"I beg your Majesty to make her let go!" the poor devil implored.

"I will not!" said the Prince. "You'll have to carry her back to earth yourself and get rid of her as best you can. Perhaps this will be a lesson to you."

So the devil, very tired and very cross, shambled back to earth with Katcha still clinging to his neck. He tried every way to get her off. He promised her wooded hills and rich meadows if she but let him go. He cajoled her, he cursed her, but all to no avail. Katcha still held on.

Breathless and discouraged he came at last to a meadow where a shepherd, wrapped in a great shaggy sheepskin coat, was tending his flocks. The devil transformed himself into an ordinary looking man so that the shepherd didn't recognize him.

"Hi, there," the shepherd said, "what's that you're carrying?"

"Don't ask me," the devil said with a sigh. "I'm so worn out I'm nearly dead. I was walking yonder not thinking of anything at all when along comes a woman and jumps on my back and won't let go. I'm trying to carry her to the nearest village to get rid of her there, but I don't believe I'm able. My legs are giving out."

The shepherd, who was a good-natured chap, said: "I tell you what: I'll help you. I can't leave my sheep long, but I'll carry her halfway."

"Oh," said the devil, "I'd be very grateful if you did!"

So the shepherd yelled at Katcha: "Hi, there, you! Catch hold of me!"

When Katcha saw that the shepherd was a handsome youth, she let go of the devil and leapt upon the shepherd's back, catching hold of the collar of his sheepskin coat.

Now the young shepherd soon found that the long shaggy coat and Katcha made a pretty heavy load for walking. In a few moments he was sick of his bargain and began casting about for some way of getting rid of Katcha.

Presently he came to a pond and he thought to himself that he'd like to throw her in. He wondered how he could do it. Perhaps he could manage it by throwing in his greatcoat with her. The coat was so loose that he thought he could slip out of it without Katcha's discovering what he was doing. Very cautiously he slipped out one arm. Katcha didn't move. He

27

slipped out the other arm. Still Katcha didn't move. He unlooped the first button. Katcha noticed nothing. He unlooped the second button. Still Katcha noticed nothing. He unlooped the third button and kerplunk! he had pitched coat and Katcha and all into the middle of the pond!

When he got back to his sheep, the devil looked at him in amazement.

"Where's Katcha?" he gasped.

"Oh," the shepherd said, pointing over his shoulder with his thumb, "I decided to leave her up yonder in a pond."

"My dear friend," the devil cried, "I thank you! You have done me a great favor. If it hadn't been for you I might be carrying Katcha till dooms-day. I'll never forget you and some time I'll reward you. As you don't know who it is you've helped, I must tell you I'm a devil."

With these words the devil vanished.

For a moment the shepherd was dazed. Then he laughed and said to himself: "Well, if they're all as stupid as he is, we ought to be able for them!"

The country where the shepherd lived was ruled over by a dissolute young duke who passed his days in riotous living and his nights in carousing. He gave over the affairs of state to two governors who were as bad as he. With extortionate taxes and unjust fines they robbed the people until the whole land was crying out against them.

Now one day for amusement the duke summoned an astrologer to court and ordered him to read in the planets the fate of himself and his two governors. When the astrologer had cast a horoscope for each of the three reprobates, he was greatly disturbed and tried to dissuade the duke from questioning him further.

"Such danger," he said, "threatens your life and the lives of your two governors that I fear to speak."

"Whatever it is," said the duke, "speak. But I warn you to speak the truth, for if what you say does not come to pass you will forfeit your life."

The astrologer bowed and said: "Hear then, O Duke, what the planets foretell: Before the second quarter of the moon, on such and such a day, at such and such an hour, a devil will come and carry off the two governors. At the full of the moon on such and such a day, at such and such an hour, the same devil will come for your Highness and carry you off to hell."

The duke pretended to be unconcerned but in his heart he was deeply shaken. The voice of the astrologer sounded to him like the voice of judgment and for the first time conscience began to trouble him.

As for the governors, they couldn't eat a bite of food and were carried from the palace half dead with fright. They piled their ill-gotten wealth into wagons and rode away to their castles, where they barred all the doors and windows in order to keep the devil out.

The duke reformed. He gave up his evil ways and corrected the abuses of state in the hope of averting if possible his cruel fate.

The poor shepherd had no inkling of any of these things. He tended his flocks from day to day and never bothered his head about the happenings in the great world.

Suddenly one day the devil appeared before him and said: "I have come, my friend, to repay you for your kindness. When the moon is in its first quarter, I was to carry off the former governors of this land because they robbed the poor and gave the duke evil counsel. However, they're behaving themselves now so they're to be given another chance. But they don't know this. Now on such and such a day do you go to the first castle where a crowd of people will be assembled. When a cry goes up and the gates open and I come dragging out the governor, do you step up to me and say: 'What do you mean by this? Get out of here or there'll be trouble!' I'll pretend to be greatly frightened and make off. Then ask the governor to pay you two bags of gold, and if he haggles just threaten to call me back. After that go on to the castle of the second governor and do the same thing and demand the same pay. I warn you, though, be prudent with the money and use it only for good. When the moon is full, I'm to carry off the duke himself, for he was so wicked that he's to have no second chance. So don't try to save him, for if you do you'll pay for it with your own skin. Don't forget!"

The shepherd remembered carefully everything the devil told him. When the moon was in its first quarter he went to the first castle. A great crowd of people was gathered outside waiting to see the devil carry away the governor.

Suddenly there was a loud cry of despair, the gates of the castle opened, and there was the devil, as black as night, dragging out the governor. He, poor man, was half dead with fright.

The shepherd elbowed his way through the crowd, took the governor by the hand, and pushed the devil roughly aside.

"What do you mean by this?" he shouted. "Get out of here or there'll be trouble!"

Instantly the devil fled and the governor fell on his knees before the shepherd and kissed his hands and begged him to state what he wanted in reward. When the shepherd asked for two bags of gold, the governor ordered that they be given him without delay.

Then the shepherd went to the castle of the second governor and went through exactly the same performance.

It goes without saying that the duke soon heard of the shepherd, for he had been anxiously awaiting the fate of the two governors. At once he sent a wagon with four horses to fetch the shepherd to the palace and when the shepherd arrived he begged him piteously to rescue him likewise from the devil's clutches.

"Master," the shepherd answered, "I cannot promise you anything. I have to consider my own safety. You have been a great sinner, but if you really want to reform, if you really want to rule your people justly and kindly and wisely as becomes a true ruler, then indeed I will help you even if I have to suffer hellfire in your place."

The duke declared that with God's help he would mend his ways and the shepherd promised to come back on the fatal day.

With grief and dread the whole country awaited the coming of the full moon. In the first place the people had greeted the astrologer's prophecy with joy, but since the duke had reformed their feelings for him had changed.

Time sped fast as time does whether joy be coming or sorrow and all too soon the fatal day arrived.

Dressed in black and pale with fright, the duke sat expecting the arrival of the devil.

Suddenly the door flew open and the devil, black as night, stood before him. He paused a moment and then he said, politely:

"Your time has come, Lord Duke, and I am here to get you!"

Without a word the duke arose and followed the devil to the courtyard, which was filled with a great multitude of people.

At that moment the shepherd, all out of breath, came pushing his way through the crowd, and ran straight at the devil, shouting out:

"What do you mean by this? Get out of here or there'll be trouble!"

"What do you mean?" whispered the devil. "Don't you remember what I told you?"

"Hush!" the shepherd whispered back. "I don't care anything about the duke. This is to warn you! You know Katcha? She's alive and she's looking for you!"

The instant the devil heard the name of Katcha he turned and fled.

All the people cheered the shepherd, while the shepherd himself laughed in his sleeve to think that he had taken in the devil so easily.

As for the duke, he was so grateful to the shepherd that he made him his chief counselor and loved him as a brother. And well he might, for the shepherd was a sensible man and always gave him sound advice.

THE WHITE DOGS OF ARRAN

FOR a long hour, on that November afternoon, my brother Ted had been standing at the gate below the ranch house, waiting and waiting, while the twilight filled the round hollow of the valley as water slowly fills a cup. At last the figure of a rider, silhouetted against the rose-colored sky, came into view along the crest of the rocky ridge. The little cow pony was loping as swiftly as the rough trail would permit, but to Ted's impatient eyes it seemed to crawl as slowly as a fly on a window pane. Although the horseman looked like a cow puncher, at that distance, with his slouch hat and big saddle, the eager boy knew that it was the district doctor making his far rounds over the range. A swift epidemic had been sweeping over Montana, passing from one ranch to another and leaving much illness and suffering behind. Ted's uncle and the cousin who was his own age had both been stricken two days before and it seemed that the doctor would never come.

"I'm glad you are here," he said as the doctor's pony, covered with foam and quivering with fatigue, passed through the open gate. "We have two patients for you."

The man nodded.

"Fever, I suppose," he commented, "and aching bones, and don't know what to make of themselves because they have never been sick before? I have seen a hundred such cases in the last few days. It is bad at all the ranches, but the sheep herders, off in their cabins by themselves, are hit particularly hard."

He slipped from the saddle and strode into the house, leaving Ted to take the tired pony around to the stables. It was very dark now and growing cold, but he felt warm and comforted, somehow, since the doctor had come. He heard running feet behind him and felt a dog's nose, cold and wet, thrust into his hand. It was Pedro, the giant, six months' old wolf hound puppy, long legged and shaggy haired, the pride of Ted's life and the best beloved of all his possessions. The big dog followed his master into the stable and sat down, blinking solemnly in the circle of lantern light, while the boy was caring for the doctor's horse and bedding it down. Ted's thoughts were very busy, now with his anxieties about his uncle, now racing out over the range to wonder how those in the stricken ranch houses and lonely cabins might be faring. There was the ranch on Arran Creek — people there were numerous enough to care for each other. It might be worse at Thompson's Crossing, and, oh, how would it be with those shepherds who lived in tiny cottages here and there along the Big Basin, so far from neighbors that often for months they saw no other faces than the wooly vacant ones of their thousands of sheep.

There was one, a big grizzled Irishman, whom Ted had seen only a few times. Nevertheless, he was one of his closest friends. They had met on a night when the boy was hunting, and he could remember still how they had lain together by the tiny camp fire, with the coyotes yelping in the distance, with the great plain stretching out into the dark, with the slender curl of smoke rising straight upward and the big stars seeming almost within reach of his hand in the thin air. The lonely Irishman had opened his heart to his new friend and had told him much of his own country, so unlike this big bare one, a dear green land where the tumbledown cottages and little fields were crowded together in such comforting comradeship.

"You could open your window of a summer night and give a call to the neighbors," he sighed, "and you needn't to have the voice of the giant Finn McCoul to make them hear. In this place a man could fall sick and die alone and no one be the wiser."

His reminiscences had wandered farther and farther until he began to tell the tales and legends familiar in his own countryside, stories of the "Little People" and of Ireland in ancient times. Of them all Ted remembered most clearly the story of the white grayhounds of the King of Connemara, upon which his friend had dwelt long, showing that in spite of its being a thousand years old, it was his favorite tale.

"Like those dogs on Arran Creek, they were perhaps," the Irishman said, "only sleeker of coat and swifter of foot, I'm thinking."

"But they couldn't be faster," Ted had objected. "The Arran dogs can catch coyotes and jack-rabbits and people have called those the quickest animals that run."

"Ah," returned the other with true Irish logic, "those Arran dogs are Russian, they tell me, and these I speak of were of Connemara, and what comes out of Ireland, you may be sure, is faster and fairer than anything else on earth."

Against such reasoning Ted had judged it impossible to argue and had dropped into silence and finally into sleep with the voices of the coyotes and the legend of the lean, white Irish grayhounds still running like swift water through his dreams.

After that he had visited the lonely shepherd whenever he could find time to travel so far. Together they had hunted deer and trapped beaver in the foothills above the Big Basin or, when the sheep had to be moved to new pasture, had spent hours in earnest talk, plodding patiently in the dust after the slow-moving flock. The long habit of silence had taken deep hold upon the Irishman, but with Ted alone he seemed willing to speak freely. It was on one of these occasions that he had given the boy the image of Saint Christopher, "For," he said, "you are like to be a great roamer and a great traveler from the way you talk, and those who carry the good Saint Christopher with them, always travel safely."

Now, as Ted thought of illness and pestilence spreading across the thinly settled state, his first and keenest apprehension was for the safety of his friend. His work done, he went quickly back to the house where the doctor was already standing on the doorstep again.

"They are not bad cases, either of them," he was saying to Ted's aunt. "If they have good care there is no danger, but if they don't—then Heaven help them, I can't."

Ted came close and pulled his sleeve.

"Tell me," he questioned quickly, "Michael Martin isn't sick, is he?"

"Michael Martin?" repeated the doctor. "A big Irishman in the cabin at the upper edge of Big Basin? Yes, he's down sick as can be, poor fellow, with no one but a gray old collie dog, about the age of himself, I should think, to keep him company."

He turned back to give a few last directions.

"I suppose you are master of the house with your uncle laid up," he said to Ted again, "and I will have to apply to you to lend me a fresh horse so that I can go on."

"You're never going on to-night?" exclaimed Ted; "why, you have been riding for all you were worth, all day!"

"Yes, and all the night before," returned the doctor cheerfully, "but this is no time to spare horses or doctors. Good gracious, boy, what's that?" For Pedro, tall and white in the dark, standing on his hind legs to insert an inquisitive puppy nose between the doctor's collar and his neck, was an unexpected and startling apparition.

"That's my dog," Ted explained proudly; "Jim McKenzie, over on Arran Creek, gave him to me; he has a lot of them, you know. Pedro is only half grown now, he is going to be a lot bigger when he is a year old. Yes, I'll bring you a horse right away, yours couldn't go another mile."

When, a few minutes later, the sound of hoofs came clattering up from the stables it seemed certain that there were more than four of them.

"What's this?" the doctor inquired, seeing a second horse with saddlebags and blanket roll strapped in place and observing Ted's boots and riding coat.

"My aunt and the girls will take care of Uncle," the boy replied, "so I am going out to see Michael Martin. You can tell me what to do for him as we ride up the trail."

They could feel the sharp wind almost before they began climbing the ridge. So far, summer had lingered into November, but the weather was plainly changing now and there had been reports of heavy snowfalls in the mountains. The stars shone dimly, as though through a veil of mist.

"You had better push on as fast as you can," advised the doctor as they came to the parting of their ways. "When a man is as sick as Michael, what ever is to happen, comes quickly." His horse jumped and snorted. "There's that white puppy of yours again. What a ghost he is! He is rather big to take with you to a sick man's cabin."

Pedro had come dashing up the trail behind them, in spite of his having been ordered sternly to stay at home. At six months old the sense of obedience is not quite so great as it should be, and the love of going on an expedition is irresistible.

"It would take me forever to drive him home now," Ted admitted; "I will take him along to Jim McKenzie's and leave him there with his brothers. I can make Arran Creek by breakfast time and ought to get to Michael's not long after noon. Well, so long!"

The stars grew more dim and the wind keener as he rode on through the night. His pony cantered steadily with the easy rocking-horse motion that came near to lulling him to sleep. Pedro paddled alongside, his long legs covering the miles with untiring energy. They stopped at midnight to drink from the stream they were crossing, to rest a little and to eat some lunch from the saddlebags. Then they pressed on once more, on and on, until gray and crimson began to show behind the mountains to the eastward, and the big white house of Arran at last came into sight.

Jim McKenzie's place was bigger than the ordinary ranch house, for there were gabled roofs showing through the group of trees, there were tall barns and a wide fenced paddock where lived the white Russian wolfhounds for which the Arran ranch was famous. A deep-voiced chorus of welcome was going up as Ted and Pedro came down the trail. The puppy responded joyfully and went bounding headlong to the foot of the slope to greet his brothers. It was a beautiful sight to see the band of great dogs, their coats like silver in the early morning light, romping together like a dozen kittens, pursuing each other in circles, checking, wheeling, rolling one another over, leaping back and forth over the low fences that divided the paddock, with the grace and free agility of deer. Early as it was, Jim McKenzie was walking down to the stables and stopped to greet Ted as, weary and dusty, he rode through the gate.

"Sure we'll keep Pedro," he said when he had heard the boy's errand. "Yes, we've a good many sick here; I'd have sent out on the range myself but there was nobody to spare. They tell me the herds of sheep are in terrible confusion, and most of the herders are down. Poor old Michael Martin, I hope you get there in time to help him. Turn your horse into the corral, we'll give you another to go on with. Now come in to breakfast." Ted snatched a hurried meal, threw his saddle upon a fresh pony, and set off again. For a long distance he could hear the lamentations of Pedro protesting loudly at the paddock gate. The way, after he passed Arran Creek, led out into the flat country of the Big Basin with the sagebrush-dotted plain stretching far ahead. It seemed that he rode endlessly and arrived nowhere, so long was the way and so unchanging the landscape. Once, as he crossed a stream, a deer rose, stamping and snorting among the low bushes, and fled away toward the hills, seeming scarcely to touch the ground as it went. Later, something quick and silent, and looking like a reddish-brown collie, leaped from the sagebrush and scudded across the trail almost under his horse's feet.

"A coyote, out in the open in daylight," he reflected, somewhat startled. "It must have been cold up in the mountains to make them so bold. That looks bad for the sheep."

It was disturbing also to see how many scattered sheep he was beginning to pass, little bands, solitary ewes with half-grown lambs trotting at their heels, adventurous yearlings straying farther and farther from their comrades. Once or twice he tried to drive them together, but owing to his haste and his inexperience with their preposterous ways, he had very little success.

"There is going to be bad weather, too," he observed as he saw the blue sky disappear beneath an overcast of gray. "I had better get on to Michael's as fast as I can."

He saw the little mud and log cabin at last, tucked away among some stunted trees near the shoulder of a low ridge. It looked deceivingly near, yet he rode and rode and could not reach it. White flakes were flying now, fitfully at first, then thicker and thicker until he could scarcely see. His growing misgivings gave place to greater and greater anxiety concerning his friend, while there ran through his mind again and again the doctor's words, "Whatever is to happen, comes quickly."

It was past noon and had begun to seem as though he had been riding forever when he breasted the final slope at last, jumped from his horse, and thundered at the cabin door. The whine of a dog answered him from within, and a faint voice, broken but still audible, told him that Michael was alive. The cabin, so it seemed to him as he entered, was a good ten degrees colder than it was outside. Poor Michael, helpless and shivering on the bunk in the corner, looked like the shrunken ghost of the giant Irishman he had known before. Ted rekindled the fire, emptied his saddlebags, piled his extra blankets upon the bed and, with a skill bred of long practice in camp cookery, set about preparing a meal. Michael was so hoarse as to be almost unable to speak and so weak that his mind wandered in the midst of a sentence, yet all of his thoughts were on the care of his sheep.

"When I felt the sickness coming on me I tried to drive them in," he whispered, "but they broke and scattered and I fell beside the trail — they must get in — snow coming — "

In an hour his fever rose again, he tossed and muttered with only fleeting intervals of consciousness. Ted had found food and shelter for his horse in the sheep shed, and had settled down to his task of anxious watching. The snow fell faster and faster so that darkness came on by mid-afternoon. He had tried to drive the old collie dog out to herd in the sheep, but the poor old creature would not leave its master and, even when pushed outside, remained whining beside the door.

"He couldn't do much anyway," sighed Ted as he let him in again. "How those coyotes yelp! I wish, after all, that I had brought Pedro."

Michael had heard the coyotes too and was striving feebly to rise from his bed.

"I must go out to them, my poor creatures," he gasped. "Those devil beasts will have driven them over the whole country before morning."

But he fell back, too weak to move farther, and was silent a long time. When he did speak it was almost aloud.

"With the cold and the snow, I'm thinking there will be worse things abroad this night than just the coyotes."

He lay very still while Ted sat beside him, beginning to feel sleepy and blinking at the firelight. Eleven o'clock, twelve, one, the slow hands of his watch pointed to the crawling hours. Michael was not asleep but he said nothing, he was listening too intently. It was after one and the boy might have been dozing, when the old man spoke again.

"Hark," he said.

For a moment Ted could hear nothing save the pat-pat of the snow against the window, but the collie dog bristled and growled as he lay upon the hearth and pricked his ears sharply. Then the boy heard it too, a faint cry and far off, not the sharp yelping of the coyotes, though that was ominous enough, but the long hungry howl of a timber wolf. Tears of weakness and terror were running down the Irishman's face.

"My poor sheep, I must save them," he cried. "What's the value of a man's life alongside of the creatures that's trusted him. Those murderers will have every one of them killed for me."

Ted jumped up quickly and bundled on his coat.

"Where's your rifle, Michael?" he asked. "I don't know much about sheep, but I will do what I can."

"The rifle?" returned Michael doubtfully. "Now, I had it on my shoulder the day I went out with the sickness on me, and it is in my mind that I did not bring it home again. But there is the little gun hanging on the nail; there's no more shells for it but there's two shots still left in the chamber."

The boy took down the rusty revolver and spun the cylinder with a practised finger.

"Two shots is right," he said, "and you have no more shells? Well, two shots may scare a wolf."

39

If Michael had been in his proper senses, Ted very well knew, he would never have permitted, without protest, such an expedition as the boy was planning. As it was, however, he lay back in his bunk again, his mind wandering off once more into feverish dreams.

"If it was in the Old Country," he muttered, "the very Little People themselves would rise up to help a man in such a plight. You could be feeling the rush of their wings in the air and could hear the cry of the fairy hounds across the hills. America is a good country, but, ah — it's not the same!"

Hoping to quiet him, Ted took the little Saint Christopher from his pocket and laid it in the sick man's hand. Then he finished strapping his big boots, opened the door and slipped out quietly. Michael scarcely noticed his going.

The snow had fallen without drifting much, nor was it yet very deep. He hurried down the slope, not quite knowing what he was to do, thinking that at least he would gather as many sheep as he could and drive them homeward. But there were no sheep to be found. Where so many had been scattered that afternoon there was now not one. The whole of the Big Basin seemed suddenly to have emptied of them. Presently, however, he found a broad trail of trampled snow which he followed, where it led along a tiny stream at the foot of the bridge. As he turned, he heard again that long, terrifying howl coming down the wind. The sheep, perverse enough to scatter to the four winds when their master sought to drive them in, had now, it seemed, gathered of their own will when so great a danger threatened. Ted came upon them at last, huddled together in a little ravine where the sparse undergrowth gave some shelter from the snow. He could just see them in the dim light, their gray compact bodies crowded close, their foolish black faces seeming to look piteously to him for help. They were very quiet, although now and then they would shift a little, stamp, and move closer. The cry of the wolf was stilled at last, but not because the fierce marauder was not drawing nearer.

Yes, as he stood watching, there slipped a swift dark shape over the opposite edge of the hollow and flung itself upon a straggling ewe on the outskirts of the flock. It was followed by a second silent shadow, and a third. The poor sheep gave only one frantic bleat, then all was still again save for the sound of a hideous snapping and tearing, of a furious struggle muffled in the soft depths of the snow. Ted raised the revolver and took careful aim, he pulled the trigger, but no explosion followed. Michael's improvidence in letting his stock dwindle to only two cartridges might be counted upon also to have let those two be damp. Helplessly the boy spun the cylinder and snapped the hammer again and again, but to no purpose.

The sheep was down now, with one of the savage hunters standing over it, another tearing at its throat while the third was slipping along the edge of the flock selecting a fresh victim. Ted's weapon was useless, yet he must do something, he could not stand and see the whole herd destroyed before his eyes. Perhaps he could frighten them away as one could coyotes: he was so angry at this senseless, brutal slaughter that he lost all sense of prudence. He waved his arms up and down and shouted at the top of his lungs. He saw the creatures drop their prey and turn to look up at him. He ran along the slope, still shouting, then, of a sudden, stepped into an unexpected hollow, lost his balance and fell headlong. One of the wolves left the flock and came creeping swiftly toward him, its belly dragging in the snow.

His cry must have carried far in the quiet of the night for it was answered from a great way off. A deep voice broke the stillness and another, the call of coursing hounds who have winded their quarry but have not yet found its trail. And mingled with the barking chorus there rose high the joyful yelp of a puppy who seeks his beloved master.

Ted, slipping in the snow, struggled to his knees and called again and again. The stealthy, approaching shadow crept a yard nearer, then paused to lift a gray muzzle and sniff the air. The second wolf, with slobbering bloody jaws, turned to listen, the flock of sheep snorted and stamped in the snow.

A minute passed, then another. The boy managed to get to his feet. Then across the edge of the hollow, white against the dark underbrush, he saw the dogs coming, a line of swift, leaping forms, huge, shaggy and beautiful, their great voices all giving tongue together. Down the slope they came like an avalanche, only one separating himself from the others for a moment to fling himself upon Ted, to lick his face in ecstatic greeting and to rub a cold nose against his cheek. That nimble puppy nose it was that had lifted the latch of a gate not too securely fastened, and so set the whole pack free. Then Pedro ran to join his brothers who were sweeping on to battle. Wolfhounds are taught to catch, not to kill their quarry, but the thirst for blood was in the hearts of the dogs of Arran that night. There was only a momentof struggle, a few choking cries, and the fight was over.

Day broke next morning, clear and bright, with the chinook blowing, the big warm wind that melts the snows and lays the white hills bare almost in an hour. Michael Martin, fallen into a proper sleep at last, woke suddenly and sat up in his bunk. He startled Ted, who, rather stiff and sore from his night's adventures, was kneeling by the fire preparing breakfast. The boy came quickly to his patient's side to inquire how he did.

"It's better I am in body," the Irishman answered; "indeed I begin to feel almost like a whole man again. But—" he shook his head sadly, "my poor wits, they're gone away entirely."

Michael sighed deeply.

"After you were gone last night," he answered, "even my wandering senses had an inkling of what a dangerous errand it was, and I got up from my bed and stumbled to the window to call you back. Yes, the sickness has made me daft entirely, for as sure as I live, I saw the white grayhounds of Connemara go over the hill. But daft or no—" he sniffed at the odor of frying bacon that rose from the hearth, "I am going to relish my breakfast this day. Eh, glory me, if there isn't another of the creatures now!"

For Pedro, once more applying a knowing muzzle to the clumsy latch, had pushed open the door and stood upon the step, wagging and apologetic, the morning sun shining behind him. Long-legged and awkward, he stepped over the threshold and came to the bedside to sniff inquisitively at the little silver image that lay on the blanket. Michael could never be persuaded to believe otherwise than that Saint Christopher had brought him.

WIND AN' WAVE AN' WANDHERIN' FLAME

("'Tis mindin' somethin' that happened far an' back o' the times o' the Little People I am. Sure, 'tis meself had nigh on forgot it entirely, but when all's quiet I'll be afther tellin' it.")

THERE was always battlin' somewhere, back in those days; an' heroes that fought with sword an' spear—forged far up an' under the rainbow by Len the Smith, that was mighty in all sorts o' wisdom.

Now one time he was beatin' out a great shield o' gold; an' 'twas wrought so cunnin' that who turned it over an' laid it on the wather could step on it an' sail where he would. An' for a device on it he made roses o' the fine gold, raised far out from it, as they'd been growin' right there. Almost they seemed wavin' in the wind.

An' as he came to sthrikin' the last blows, his hand slipped, an' his great hammer went flyin' downward through the air; an' his cry o' command sent ringin' afther it was too late to hindher.

Now 'twas about toward sunset, an' the waves were beatin' high an' wild afther storm on the west coast, that Artan, son o' Duallach, that was a king's son, was huntin' along the coast. All day he'd been tryin' to keep from the company o' Myrdu, his half-brother, but only by now had he shaken him off; an' he was runnin' swiftly, for gladness o' bein' alone with the breeze an' the flyin' spray.

Just as the sinkin' sun touched the sea, he heard the great cryin'-out o' Len, out o' the North, an' looked up into the deep sky. An' there he saw, whirlin' down toward him, somethin' first dark an' then bright. Not a fearin' thought was in him; an' as it came nigh he sprang with hand stretched out an' caught it —just savin' it from bein' buried in the beach sand.

The force of its fallin' sent him to his knees, but in a breath he was on his feet again, lookin' at what he held. Sure, 'twas nothin' less than a great hammer, glowin' an' darkenin' by turns, as there had been livin' fire within it.

"What'n ever are ye, then?" cried Artan, out o' the surprise, never thinkin' on gettin' an answer. Yet thrue an' at once came a whisperin' like wind in pine forests far off—

"The hammer o' Len."

"An' how'll I get ye back to him, not knowin' where to find him?" asked Artan. "Sure, the winds must rise up an' blow me to the end o' the rainbow, where he sits, or I'll never get there at all."

The words were scarce past his lips when down across the hills came a warm gust o' south wind—the last o' the storm—an' caught him up, still clingin' to the hammer, an' swept him upwards till he could see naught for mist an' hurryin' clouds. Then came a feelin' o' sinkin', an' a sudden jar; an' there he was standin' on green turf, lookin' at white mountains, risin' higher nor aught he'd seen, an' between him an' them shimmered the rainbow itself, glowin' all colors in the light o' sunset.

"Ay, 'tis aisy seein' where I am," laughed Artan, startin' toward it bravely.

For a while he went on, an' at last he came nigh enough to see the mighty shape o' Len, standin' waitin' at his forge. An' while night was fast comin' on, an' the stars showin' out in the sky over all, yet the sunfire was still flamin' up in his smithy, workin' his will at a word.

If fear had had place in the heart of Artan, then was time for it, when he saw the deep eyes o' Len, like dark sea-water in caves, lookin' far an' through him. But never had that come to him, an' without speakin' he raised the hammer toward the sthrong knotted hand that claimed it.

"Whist, then!" says Len, graspin' it quick for fear the metal was coolin'. "Say naught till I'm done!" With that he beat an' turned the shield, an' gave the endin' touches to it. Then, with another big shout, he hung it on the rainbow, flashin' an' shinin' till men on earth below saw it for Northern Lights in the night sky.

"How came ye here in me forge, Artan, son o' Duallach?" he cried.

"That I know not," spoke out Artan. "When I held yon hammer in hand, an' cried on the wind for blowin' me to him that owned it—for no other road there was for returnin' it — the warm blast came out o' the south an' caught me up here."

"Ay," laughed Len, deep an' hearty. "The winds are at the will o' him that handles it; but too great a power is that to be given careless to mortal man. What reward will ye have, now? Whether gold, or power above other men, or the fairest o' maids for yer wife?"

Then the blood reddened the face of Artan.

"Naught care I for gold," says he. "An' power over men should be for him that wins it fair."

"Then 'tis the fairest o' maids ye'll be afther wantin'?" asked Len. "Have ye seen such a one?"

"Nay," says Artan. "Dark are the faces in the house o' Duallach, an' little to me likin'."

"Then shall ye have one fair as day," says Len. He turned to where the shield was hangin', an' from the heart o' that same he plucked a rose o' the beaten gold, an' gave it to Artan.

"Cast it in the sea surf at sunrise," says he, "callin' 'Darthuil!' — then shall ye have yer reward. But one thing mind. Safely yer own is she not till first lost an' won back. When ye know not where to seek aid in searchin', cry on me name at the sea-coast, an' aid will there be for ye if ye come not too late — wind, wave, an' wandherin' flame. Never does Len forget. Hold fast yer rose."

As he spoke, again came a gale, chill from the north this time, an' whirled Artan past cloud an' above surgin' seas, an' left him on the hilltop above the beach at the last hour before the dawnin'.

Quick Artan hastened down the cliff, still graspin' the golden rose, an' stood where the little small waves curled over the stones, waitin' for the first gleam o' the sun to touch the sea. Hours it seemed to him, but minutes it was in truth, before he caught a long breath, raised the rose high in air, an' tossed it swift an' sure into the snowy crest of a green incomin' wave.

"Darthuil!" he cried, an' the cliff echo made a song of it.

As the drops flew upward in the red dawn an' the breaker swept in, there by his side stood a maid with the gold o' the rose in her hair, an' the white o' sea-foam in her fair skin, an' the color o' the sunrise in lips an' cheek. Blither nor spring, he caught her hand an' led her over the hills to the house o' Duallach, they two singin' for joy o' livin' as they went.

Now not long had the two been wed (an' welcome were they under the roof of Duallach), when Myrdu, that was half-brother to Artan, but older nor him, came back from far huntin', ill-pleased at missin' Artan for his companion, an' for helpin' him carry the red deer he'd shot.

"'Tis an ill youth," says he, "an' will get no good from lyin' on the cliff edge an' lettin' the hunt go by."

"Nay," says Duallach, slow to anger. "Fair fortune has he won, an' the favor o' the gods; an' has brought home a bride, fair as the sun at noon."

Then was Myrdu half ragin' from bein' jealous; but not wishin' to show that same, he called for meat an' dhrink to be brought him in the great hall. An' Artan, wishin' to be friendly like, cried out for Darthuil to serve his brother. Sure, when Myrdu saw her comin' toward him — shinin' among the dark lasses o' Duallach's household like a star in the night sky — fury was in his heart for thinkin' that Artan, bein' younger nor him, had won what he had not, an' soon he laid plans for stealin' her from his brother.

'Twas not many days before word o' this came to the ear o' Duallach; an' he, hatin' strife, bade Artan an' Darthuil take horse an' ride swiftly southward to the Lough o' the Lone Valley, to dwell on the little island in it till evil wishes had passed from the heart o' Myrdu. So Artan, mindin' what Len had foretold, yet thinkin' it wiser not to be afther losin' Darthuil at all, rode away with her on his left hand when Myrdu was sleepin' an' not knowin' what was bein' done.

When he roused an' found them gone, an' that none o' the house would say whither, he was in a fine passion; but he made as if he was afther goin' huntin', an' took his two fierce hounds an' went off to trace the road they'd taken. An' sure enough, 'twas not many hours before he was on their path.

Now safer would it have been had Artan told Darthuil the full raison why he was takin' her far into the shelter o' forest an' lough o' the wildherness; but she, trustin' him, asked naught, thinkin' no evil o' livin' man. So scarce had Artan left her in the low cabin on the island an' gone off to hunt, than Myrdu pushed through the bushes, leavin' the hounds on the shore behind, an' floated himself out to the island on a couple o' logs lashed with a thong o' deer-skin. Ay, but Darthuil was startled, not dhreamin' why he'd come.

"'Tis Artan is hurt, an' afther sendin' me for ye," says Myrdu, lookin' down unaisy like, from not wishin' to meet the rare clear eyes o' her. "Come, an' I'll take ye where he lies."

Not waitin' a moment was Darthuil, then, but hurried doin' as she was bid, never thinkin' what evil might be in store.

Afther a few hours Artan came back through the trees, an' game a plenty he'd found. He pulled out his boat o' skins, an' quick paddled back to the island. But there he found no Darthuil; no, nor any sign o' her save the little print o' her sandal by the wather's edge.

Then came to his mind the promise o' Len. Never darin' to waste an hour searchin' by himself, he ferried his horse across to the mainland, mounted, an' pushed for the sea. Never once did he stop for restin' till he was standin' where the waves beat over him, where he had cried on Darthuil, an' she had come to him.

"Len!" he called. "Yer aidin', Len! Darthuil is stolen from me."

There came a rumblin' o' thunder, an' on the shore stood a great figure, like a pillar o' cloud reachin' half to the sky.

"Never safe yer own till lost an' found, I said," came the deep voice. "Now I give ye wild servants, a wind an' a wave an' a wandherin' flame for helpin' ye to bring her safe again. Mind well that each will obey ye but once, so call on them only when yer sharpest need comes. When ye've again set the feet o' Darthuil safe in the hall o' Duallach, none can take her from ye more. Now follow yer love. 'Tis to the Northland has Myrdu carried her. Let him not pass the White Rocks, or wind an' wave an' flame will lose power to aid ye. Use yer wit, now, an' use it well."

Artan would have spoken to thank him, but with the last word Len was no more there; so he mounted again an' turned to the north; an' behind him came the wind, whisperin' over the grass; an' the wave, runnin' up the sthream near at hand; an' the flame, creepin' among dhry leaves, but settin' fire to naught else, its time not bein' come.

Together they all thraveled the betther part of a long day, an' late on Artan saw dust risin' ahead. 'Twas a cloud that Myrdu had raised to hide the way he was goin', an' beyond it he was ridin', carryin' Darthuil before him on his saddle o' skins, with the two hounds lopin' along beside to fright her from tryin' to escape, an' to give warnin' of any followin'; while not many miles ahead were the White Rocks, that he was pushin' to reach.

On hurried Artan, but his horse was wearied, an' little head could he make. Moreover, the cloud o' dust left him uncertain o' what was hid. So he thought well, an' chose wind to serve him first.

"Go on, an' blow the dust far away, whisperin' courage to Darthuil the while," says he. An' at once the wind sped far ahead, obeyin' his command. When the two dogs felt it touch them, they cowered low; but Darthuil took heart, knowin' that help was at hand. An' the dust was no more hidin' her from Artan, so she waved her hand an' called aloud to him to ride in haste.

Then Myrdu, fearin' that he might yet lose her, threw a handful o' twigs behind him in the road; an' fallin' they turned into dead trees, stoppin' the way on all sides. But Artan well knew the way to clear his path.

"Go forward!" he cried to the wandherin' flame, "an' leave not a trace o' them!" As he spoke, the flame swept up high in air, roarin' an' smokin'; an' in half an instant naught remained o' the logs but a pile o' smoldherin' ashes. But still was Myrdu fast nearin' his goal, an' had one thing more for helpin'.

He dropped a little sharp knife in the roadway; an' as it fell, it cut into the dust, an' there opened a wide, terrible chasm, not to be crossed by horse nor man. Then Artan grew clear desperate.

"Wave!" he shouted, "bring Darthuil to me!"

Up then it rose, rollin' forward like flood-tide in spring; an' it filled the gulf, an' swept away dogs an' horse an' Myrdu himself, that none were heard of from that on; but Darthuil it floated gentle like, as she had been a tuft o' thistle-down, back to Artan, waitin' for her.

He caught her an' clasped her close, an' turned his horse, an' never halted till he led her safe into the hall o' Duallach, where none might steal her from him again. An' there they lived happy all their lives.

But as for the wind an' the wave an' the wandherin' flame, so sweet an' fair was Darthuil that ne'er would they go from her to return to Len. To the last o' her life the wind blew soft for her when 'twas overly hot elsewhere, an' clear cool wather flowed up from the ground to save her dhrawin' any from the river, an' fire burned bright on her hearth without need o' plenishin'; an' all that for the love o' Darthuil, that was made by Len out o' the foam tossed by the wind from the sea-wave, an' the wandherin' flame o' the sunrise.

THE KING, THE QUEEN, AND THE BEE

ON a bright summer's day, when the sun beat down fiercely upon the heads of the people, King Solomon sought the shade of one of his favorite gardens. But even where the foliage on the trees was so thick that it seemed the sun's rays could not penetrate, it was also hot. Not a breath of air was there to fan the monarch's cheek, and he lay down on the thick grass and gazed through the branches of the trees at the blue sky.

"This great heat makes me weary," said the King, and in a few minutes he had quietly fallen into a deep sleep.

All was still in the beautiful garden, except for the sound of a few humming birds, the twittering of the moths whose many-colored wings looked more beautiful than ever in the bright sunshine, and the buzzing of the bees. But even these sounds grew still as the fierce rays from the sky grew hotter until all nature seemed hushed to rest. Only one tiny bee was left moving in the garden. It flew steadily from flower to flower, sipping the honey, until at length it began to feel overcome by the heat.

"Oh, dear! I wonder what is the matter with me," buzzed the little bee. "This is the first time I have come out of the hive, and I do feel queer. I hope I am not going to faint."

The little bee felt giddy, and after flying round and round dizzily for a few minutes it fell and dropped right on to King Solomon's nose. Immediately the King awoke with such a start that the little bee was frightened almost out of its wits and flew straight back to the hive.

King Solomon sat up and looked round to see what it was that had awakened him so rudely. He felt a strange pain at the tip of his nose. He rubbed it with his royal forefinger, but the pain increased.

Attendants came rushing towards him and asked him what was the matter.

"I must have been stung on the nose by a bee," said the King angrily. "Send for the Lord High Physician and the Keeper of the Court Plaister immediately. I cannot have a blister on the tip of my nose. To-morrow I am to be visited by the Queen of Sheba, and it will not do to have a swollen nose tied up in a sling."

The Lord High Physician came with his many assistants, each carrying a box of ointment, or lint, or some other preparation which might be required. King Solomon's nose, and especially the tip of it, was examined most carefully through a microscope.

"It is almost nothing," said the Lord High Physician reassuringly. "It is just a tiny sting from a very little bee which did not leave its sting in the wound. It will be healed in an hour or two and the Queen of Sheba will not be able to notice that anything at all is the matter to-morrow."

"But meanwhile it smarts," said King Solomon. "I am seriously annoyed with the little bee. How dared it sting me, King Solomon, monarch of all living things on earth, in the air and in the waters. Knows it not that I am its Royal Master to whom all homage and respect is due?"

The pain soon ceased, but His Majesty did not like the smell of the greasy ointment which was put on his nose, and he determined that the bee should be brought before him for trial.

"Place the impudent little bee under arrest at once," he commanded, "and bring it before me so that I may hear what it has to say."

"But I know it not," returned the Lord High Chamberlain, to whom the command was given.

"Then summon the Queen bee before me in an hour and bid her bring the culprit," answered the monarch. "Tell her that I shall hold all the bees guilty until the saucy little offender is produced before me."

The order was carried to the hive by one of the butterflies in attendance on the King and spread consternation among the bees. Such a buzzing there was that the butterfly said:

"Stop making that noise. If the King hears you, it will only make matters worse."

The Queen bee promised to obey King Solomon's command, and in an hour she made her appearance in state before the great throne. Slowly and with much pomp, the Queen bee made her way to King Solomon. She was the largest of the bees and was escorted by a bodyguard of twelve female bees who cleared the way before her, walking backwards and bowing constantly with their faces to her.

King Solomon was surrounded by all his Court which included living beings, fairies, demons, spirits, goblins, animals, birds and insects. All raised their voices in a loud hurrah when His Majesty took his seat on the Throne, and a very strange noise the Court made.The lions roared, the serpents hissed, the birds chirped, the fairies sang and the demons howled. The goblins that had no voices could only grin.

"Silence!" cried a herald. "The Queen bee is requested to stand forth."

Still attended by her twelve guards, the Queen bee approached the foot of the Throne and made obeisance to King Solomon.

"I, thy slave, the Queen bee," she buzzed, "am here at thy bidding, mighty ruler, great and wise. Command and thou shalt be obeyed."

"It is well," replied Solomon. "Hast thou brought with thee the culprit, the bee that did dare to attack my nose with its sting?"

"I have, your Majesty," answered the Queen bee. "It is a young bee that this day did leave the hive for the first time. It has confessed to me. It did not attack your Majesty wilfully, but by accident, owing to giddiness caused by the heat, and it could not have injured your Majesty seriously, because it left not its sting in the wound. Be merciful, gracious King."

"Fear not my judgment," said the King. "Bid the bee stand forth."

Tremblingly, the little bee stood at the foot of the Throne and bowed three times to King Solomon.

"Knowest thou not," said the King, "that I am thy royal master whose person must be held sacred by all living things?"

"Yes, gracious Majesty," buzzed the bee. "Thy slave is aware of this. It was but an accident, and it is the nature of thy slave, the bee, who is in duty bound to obey thy laws, to thrust forth its sting when in danger. I thought I was in danger when I fell."

"So was I, for I was beneath you," returned King Solomon.

"Punish me not," pleaded the bee. "I am but one of your Majesty's smallest and humblest slaves, but even I may be of service to your Majesty some day."

These words from the little bee made the whole Court laugh. Even the goblins which could not speak grinned from ear to ear and rolled their big eyes.

"Silence!" commanded the King sternly. "There is naught to laugh at in the bee's answer. It pleases me well. Go, thou art free. Some day I may need thee."

The little bee bowed its head three times before the King and flew away, buzzing happily.

Next day it kept quite close to the Palace.

"I want to see the procession when the Queen of Sheba arrives," it said, "and I also must be near the King in case His Majesty may want me."

In great state, the beautiful Queen of Sheba, followed by hundreds of handsomely robed attendants, approached King Solomon who was seated on his Throne, surrounded by all his Court.

"Great and mighty King of Israel," she said, curtseying low, "I have heard of thy great wisdom and would fain put it to the test. Hitherto all questions put to thee hast thou answered without difficulty. But I have sworn to puzzle thy wondrous wisdom with my woman's wit. Be heedful."

"Beauteous Queen of Sheba," returned King Solomon, rising and bowing in return to her curtsey, "thou art as witty as thou art fair, and if thou art successful in puzzling me, thy triumph shall be duly rewarded. I will load thee with rich presents and proclaim thy wit and wisdom to the whole world."

"I accept thy challenge," replied the Queen, "and at once."

Behind Her Majesty stood two beautiful girl attendants, each holding a bouquet of flowers. The Queen of Sheba took the flowers, and holding a bouquet in each hand, said to King Solomon:

"Tell me, thou who art the wisest man on earth, which of these bunches of flowers is real and which artificial."

"They are both beautiful and their fragrance delicious in the extreme," replied King Solomon.

"Ah," said the Queen, "but only one bunch has fragrance. Which is it?"

King Solomon looked at the flowers. Both bunches looked exactly alike. From where he sat, it was impossible to detect any difference. He did not answer at once, and he knit his brows as if perplexed. The courtiers also looked troubled. Never before had they seen the King hesitate.

"Is it impossible for your Majesty to answer the question?" the Queen asked.

Solomon shook his head and smiled.

"Never yet has a problem baffled me," he said. "Your Majesty shall be answered, and correctly."

"And at once," said the Queen of Sheba imperiously.

"So be it," answered King Solomon, gazing thoughtfully round and raising his magic scepter.

Immediately he heard what no one else did, the faint buzzing of the tiny wings of the little bee which had settled on one of the window panes of the Palace.

"Bid that window be opened," he commanded, pointing to it with his scepter, "and let the bee enter to obey my wish."

The window was promptly opened, and in flew the little bee. Straight towards the Queen of Sheba it flew, and now its buzzing could be heard by all the courtiers, who eagerly watched its flight through the air. Without any hesitation, it settled on the bouquet in the Queen's left hand.

"Thou hast my answer, fair Queen of Sheba," said King Solomon, rising, "given to thee by one of the tiniest of my subjects. It has settled on the flowers that are natural. The bouquet in your right hand is made by human hands."

The whole Court applauded the monarch's wisdom in bidding the little bee help him out of his difficulty.

"Your Majesty is indeed the wisest man on earth," said the Queen.

"Thanks, my little friend," said the King to the bee, and it flew away, buzzing merrily.

THE WELL OF THE WORLD'S END

ONCE upon a time, and a very good time it was, though it wasn't in my time, nor in your time, nor in any one else's time, there was a girl whose mother had died, and her father married again. And her stepmother hated her because she was more beautiful than herself, and she was very cruel to her. She used to make her do all the servant's work, and never let her have any peace.

At last, one day, the stepmother thought to get rid of her altogether; so she handed her a sieve and said to her: "Go, fill it at the Well of the World's End and bring it home to me full, or woe betide you." For she thought she would never be able to find the Well of the World's End, and, if she did, how could she bring home a sieve full of water?

Well, the girl started off, and asked every one she met to tell her where was the Well of the World's End. But nobody knew, and she didn't know what to do, when a queer little old woman, all bent double, told her where it was, and how she could get to it. So she did what the old woman told her, and at last arrived at the Well of the World's End. But when she dipped the sieve in the cold, cold water, it all ran out again. She tried and she tried again, but every time it was the same; and at last she sat down and cried as if her heart would break.

Suddenly she heard a croaking voice, and she looked up and saw a great frog with goggle eyes looking at her and speaking to her.

"What's the matter, dearie?" it said.

"Oh, dear, oh, dear," she said, "my stepmother has sent me all this long way to fill this sieve with water from the Well of the World's End, and I can't fill it no how at all."

"Well," said the frog, "if you promise me to do whatever I bid you for a whole night long, I'll tell you how to fill it."

So the girl agreed, and the frog said:

"Stop it with moss and daub it with clay,

And then it will carry the water away";

and then it gave a hop, skip, and a jump, and went flop into the Well of the World's End.

So the girl looked about for some moss, and lined the bottom of the sieve with it, and over that she put some clay, and then she dipped it once again into the Well of the World's End; and this time the water didn't run out, and she turned to go away.

Just then the frog popped up its head out of the Well of the World's End, and said: "Remember your promise."

"All right," said the girl; for, thought she, "what harm can a frog do me?"

So she went back to her stepmother, and brought the sieve full of water from the Well of the World's End. The stepmother was angry as angry, but she said nothing at all.

That very evening they heard something tap-tapping at the door low down, and a voice cried out:

"Open the door, my hinny, my heart,

Open the door, my own darling;

Mind you the words that you and I spoke,

Down in the meadow, at the World's End Well."

"Whatever can that be?" cried out the stepmother, and the girl had to tell her all about it, and what she had promised the frog.

"Girls must keep their promises," said the stepmother. "Go and open the door this instant." For she was glad the girl would have to obey a nasty frog.

So the girl went and opened the door, and there was the frog from the Well of the World's End. And it hopped, and it hopped, and it jumped, till it reached the girl, and then it said:

"Lift me to your knee, my hinny, my heart;

Lift me to your knee, my own darling;

Remember the words you and I spake,

Down in the meadow by the World's End Well."

But the girl didn't like to, till her stepmother said: "Lift it up this instant, you hussy! Girls must keep their promises!"

So at last she lifted the frog up on to her lap, and it lay there for a time, till at last it said:

"Give me some supper, my hinny, my heart,

Give me some supper, my darling;

Remember the words you and I spake,

In the meadow, by the Well of the World's End."

Well, she didn't mind doing that, so she got it a bowl of milk and bread, and fed it well. And when the frog had finished, it said:

"Go with me to bed, my hinny, my heart,

Go with me to bed, my own darling;

Mind you the words you spake to me,

Down by the cold well, so weary."

But that the girl wouldn't do, till her stepmother said: "Do what you promised, girl; girls must keep their promises. Do what you're bid, or out you go, you and your froggie."

So the girl took the frog with her to bed, and kept it as far away from her as she could. Well, just as the day was beginning to break what should the frog say but:

"Chop off my head, my hinny, my heart,

Chop off my head, my own darling;

Remember the promise you made to me,

Down by the cold well so weary."

At first the girl wouldn't, for she thought of what the frog had done for her at the Well of the World's End. But when the frog said the words over again, she went and took an ax and chopped off its head, and lo! and

58

behold, there stood before her a handsome young prince, who told her that he had been enchanted by a wicked magician, and he could never be unspelled till some girl would do his bidding for a whole night, and chop off his head at the end of it.

The stepmother was surprised indeed when she found the young prince instead of the nasty frog, and she wasn't best pleased, you may be sure, when the prince told her that he was going to marry her stepdaughter because she had unspelled him. But married they were, and went away to live in the castle of the king, his father, and all the stepmother had to console her was, that it was all through her that her stepdaughter was married to a prince.

WINGS

A PEASANT girl was feeding geese, and she wept. The farmer's daughter came by and asked, "What are you blubbering about?"

"I haven't got any wings," cried the peasant girl. "Oh, I wish I could grow some wings."

"You stupid!" said the farmer's daughter. "Of course you haven't got wings. What do you want wings for?"

"I want to fly up into the sky and sing my little songs there," answered the little peasant girl.

Then the farmer's daughter was angry, and said again, "You stupid! How can you ever expect to grow wings? Your father's only a farm-laborer. They might grow on me, but not on you."

When the farmer's daughter had said that, she went away to the well, sprinkled some water on her shoulders, and stood out among the vegetables in the garden, waiting for her wings to sprout. She really believed the sun would bring them out quite soon.

But in a little while a merchant's daughter came along the road and called out to the girl who was trying to grow wings in the garden, "What are you doing standing out there, red face?"

"I am growing wings," said the farmer's daughter. "I want to fly."

Then the merchant's daughter laughed loudly, and cried out, "You stupid farm-girl; if you had wings they would only be a weight on your back."

The merchant's daughter thought she knew who was most likely to grow wings. And when she went back to the town where she lived she bought some olive-oil and rubbed it on her shoulders, and went out into the garden and waited for her wings to grow.

By and by a young lady of the Court came along, and said to her, "What are you doing out there, my child?"

When the tradesman's daughter said that she was growing wings, the young lady's face flushed and she looked quite vexed.

"That's not for you to do," she said. "It is only real ladies who can grow wings."

And she went on home, and when she got indoors she filled a tub with milk and bathed herself in it, and then went into her garden and stood in the sun and waited for her wings to come out. Presently a princess passed by the garden, and when she saw the young lady standing there she sent a servant to inquire what she was doing. The servant came back and told her that as the young lady had wanted to be able to fly she had bathed herself in milk and was waiting for her wings to grow.

The princess laughed scornfully and exclaimed, "What a foolish girl! She's giving herself trouble for nothing. No one who is not a princess can ever grow wings."

The princess turned the matter over in her mind, and when she arrived at her father's palace she went into her chamber, anointed herself with sweet-smelling perfumes, and then went down into the palace garden to wait for her wings to come.

Very soon all the young girls in the country round about went out into their gardens and stood among the vegetables so that they might get wings.

The Fairy of the Wings heard about this strange happening and she flew down to earth, and, looking at the waiting girls, she said, "If I give you all wings and let you all go flying into the sky, who will want to stay at home to cook the porridge and look after the children? I had better give wings only to one of you, namely, to her who wanted them first of all."

So wings grew from the little peasant girl's shoulders, and she was able to fly up into the sky and sing.

CHRISTMAS STORIES
THE CHRISTMAS CUCKOO

IN an old time, long ago, when the fairies were in the world, there lived a little girl so uncommonly fair and pleasant of look, that they called her Snowflower. This girl was good as well as pretty. No one had ever seen her frown or heard her say a cross word, and young and old were glad when they saw her coming.

Snowflower had no relation in the world but a very old grandmother. . . . Every evening, when the fire was heaped with the sticks she had gathered till it blazed and crackled up the cottage chimney, Dame Frostyface set aside her wheel, and told her a new story. Often did the little girl wonder where her grandmother had gathered so many stories, but she soon learned that. One sunny morning, at the time of the swallows' coming, the dame rose up, put on the gray hood and mantle in which she carried her yarn to the fairs, and said, "My child, I am going a long journey to visit an aunt of mine, who lives far in the north country. I cannot take you with me, because my aunt is the crossest woman alive, and never liked young people: but the hens will lay eggs for you; there is barley-meal in the barrel; and, as you have been a good girl, I'll tell you what to do when you feel lonely. Lay your head gently down on the cushion of the arm-chair, and say, 'Chair of my grandmother, tell me a story.' It was made by a cunning fairy, who lived in the forest when I was young, and she gave it to me because she knew nobody could keep what they got hold of better. Remember, you must never ask a story more than once in the day; and if there be any occasion to travel, you have only to seat yourself in it, and say, 'Chair of my grandmother, take me such a way.' It will carry you wherever you wish; but mind to oil the wheels before you set out, for I have sat on it these forty years in that same corner."

Having said this, Dame Frostyface set forth to see her aunt in the north country. Snowflower gathered firing and looked after the hens and cat as usual. She baked herself a cake or two of the barley-meal; but when the evening fell the cottage looked lonely. Then Snowflower remembered her grandmother's words, and, laying her head gently down, she said, "Chair of my grandmother, tell me a story."

Scarce were the words spoken, when a clear voice from under the velvet cushion . . . said: "Listen to the story of the Christmas Cuckoo!"

"Once upon a time there stood in the midst of a bleak moor, in the north country, a certain village; all its inhabitants were poor, for their fields were barren, and they had little trade, but the poorest of them all were two brothers called Scrub and Spare, who followed the cobbler's craft, and had but one stall between them. It was a hut built of clay and wattles. The door was low and always open, for there was no window. The roof did not entirely keep out the rain, and the only thing comfortable about it was a wide hearth, for which the brothers could never find wood enough to make a sufficient fire. There they worked in most brotherly friendship, though with little encouragement.

"The people of that village were not extravagant in shoes, and better cobblers than Scrub and Spare might be found. Spiteful people said there were no shoes so bad that they would not be worse for their mending. Nevertheless Scrub and Spare managed to live between their own trade, a small barley field, and a cottage garden, till one unlucky day when a new cobbler arrived in the village. He had lived in the capital city of the kingdom, and, by his own account, cobbled for the queen and the princesses. His awls were sharp, his lasts were new; he set up his stall in a neat cottage with two windows. The villagers soon found out that one patch of his would wear two of the brothers'. In short, all the mending left Scrub and Spare, and went to the new cobbler. The season had been wet and cold, their barley did not ripen well, and the cabbages never half closed in the garden. So the brothers were poor that winter, and when Christmas came they had nothing to feast on but a barley loaf, a piece of rusty bacon, and some small beer of their own brewing. Worse than that, the snow was very deep, and they could get no firewood. Their hut stood at the end of the village, beyond it spread the bleak moor, now all white and silent; but that moor had once been a forest, great roots of old trees were still to be found in it, loosened from the soil and laid bare by the winds and rains — one of these, a rough gnarled log, lay hard by their door, the half of it above the snow, and Spare said to his brother:

"'Shall we sit here cold on Christmas while the great root lies yonder? Let us chop it up for firewood, the work will make us warm.'

"'No,' said Scrub; 'it's not right to chop wood on Christmas; besides, that root is too hard to be broken with any hatchet.'

"'Hard or not we must have a fire,' replied Spare. 'Come, brother, help me in with it. Poor as we are, there is nobody in the village will have such a yule log as ours.'

"Scrub liked a little grandeur, and in hopes of having a fine yule log, both brothers strained and strove with all their might till, between pulling and pushing, the great old root was safe on the hearth, and beginning to crackle and blaze with the red embers. In high glee, the cobblers sat down to their beer and bacon. The door was shut, for there was nothing but cold moonlight and snow outside; but the hut, strewn with fir boughs, and ornamented with holly, looked cheerful as the ruddy blaze flared up and rejoiced their hearts.

"'Long life and good fortune to ourselves, brother!' said Spare. 'I hope you will drink that toast, and may we never have a worse fire on Christmas — but what is that?'

"Spare set down the drinking-horn, and the brothers listened astonished, for out of the blazing root they heard, 'Cuckoo! cuckoo!' as plain as ever the spring-bird's voice came over the moor on a May morning.

"'It is something bad,' said Scrub, terribly frightened.

"'May be not,' said Spare; and out of the deep hole at the side which the fire had not reached flew a large gray cuckoo, and lit on the table before them. Much as the cobblers had been surprised, they were still more so when it said:

"'Good gentlemen, what season is this?'

"'It's Christmas,' said Spare.

"'Then a merry Christmas to you!' said the cuckoo. 'I went to sleep in the hollow of that old root one evening last summer, and never woke till the heat of your fire made me think it was summer again; but now since you have burned my lodging, let me stay in your hut till the spring comes around — I only want a hole to sleep in, and when I go on my travels next summer be assured I will bring you some present for your trouble.'

"'Stay, and welcome,' said Spare, while Scrub sat wondering if it were something bad or not; 'I'll make you a good warm hole in the thatch. But you must be hungry after that long sleep? — here is a slice of barley bread. Come help us to keep Christmas!'

"The cuckoo ate up the slice, drank water from the brown jug, for he would take no beer, and flew into a snug hole which Spare scooped for him in the thatch of the hut.

"Scrub said he was afraid it wouldn't be lucky; but as it slept on and the days passed he forgot his fears. So the snow melted, the heavy rains came, the cold grew less, the days lengthened, and one sunny morning the brothers were awakened by the cuckoo shouting its own cry to let them know the spring had come.

"'Now I'm going on my travels,' said the bird, 'over the world to tell men of the spring. There is no country where trees bud or flowers bloom, that I will not cry in before the year goes round. Give me another slice of barley bread to keep me on my journey, and tell me what present I shall bring you at the twelvemonth's end.'

"Scrub would have been angry with his brother for cutting so large a slice, their store of barley-meal being low; but his mind was occupied with what present would be most prudent to ask: at length a lucky thought struck him.

"'Good master cuckoo,' said he, 'if a great traveler who sees all the world like you, could know of any place where diamonds or pearls were to be found, one of a tolerable size brought in your beak would help such poor men as my brother and I to provide something better than barley bread for your next entertainment.'

"'I know nothing of diamonds or pearls,' said the cuckoo; 'they are in the hearts of rocks and the sands of rivers. My knowledge is only of that which grows on the earth. But there are two trees hard by the well that lies at the world's end—one of them is called the golden tree, for its leaves are all of beaten gold: every winter they fall into the well with a sound like scattered coin and I know not what becomes of them. As for the other, it is always green like a laurel. Some call it the wise, and some the merry tree. Its leaves never fall, but they that get one of them keep a blithe heart in spite of all misfortunes, and can make themselves as merry in a hut as in a palace.'

"'Good master cuckoo, bring me a leaf off that tree,' cried Spare.

"'Now, brother, don't be a fool!' said Scrub. 'Think of the leaves of beaten gold! Dear master cuckoo, bring me one of them!'

"Before another word could be spoken, the cuckoo had flown out of the open door, and was shouting its spring cry over moor and meadow. The brothers were poorer than ever that year; nobody would send them a single shoe to mend. The new cobbler said, in scorn, they should come to be his apprentices; and Scrub and Spare would have left the village but for their barley field, their cabbage garden, and a certain maid called Fairfeather, whom both the cobblers had courted for seven years without even knowing which she meant to favor.

"Sometimes Fairfeather seemed inclined to Scrub, sometimes she smiled on Spare; but the brothers never disputed for that. They sowed their barley, planted their cabbage, and now that their trade was gone, worked in the rich villagers' fields to make out a scanty living. So the seasons came and passed: spring, summer, harvest, and winter followed each other as they have done from the beginning. At the end of the latter, Scrub and Spare had grown so poor and ragged that Fairfeather thought them beneath her notice. Old neighbors forgot to invite them to wedding feasts or merrymaking; and they thought the cuckoo had forgotten them too, when at daybreak, on the first of April, they heard a hard beak knocking at their door, and a voice crying:

"'Cuckoo! cuckoo! Let me in with my presents.'

"Spare ran to open the door, and in came the cuckoo, carrying on one side of his bill a golden leaf larger than that of any tree in the north country; and in the other, one like that of the common laurel, only it had a fresher green.

"'Here,' it said, giving the gold to Scrub and the green to Spare, 'it is a long carriage from the world's end. Give me a slice of barley bread, for I must tell the north country that the spring has come.'

"Scrub did not grudge the thickness of that slice, though it was cut from their last loaf. So much gold had never been in the cobbler's hands before, and he could not help exulting over his brother.

"'See the wisdom of my choice!' he said, holding up the large leaf of gold. 'As for yours, as good might be plucked from any hedge. I wonder a sensible bird would carry the like so far.'

"'Good master cobbler,' cried the cuckoo, finishing the slice, 'your conclusions are more hasty than courteous. If your brother be disappointed this time, I go on the same journey every year, and for your hospitable entertainment will think it no trouble to bring each of you whichever leaf you desire.'

"'Darling cuckoo!' cried Scrub, 'bring me a golden one;' and Spare, looking up from the green leaf on which he gazed as though it were a crown-jewel, said:

"'Be sure to bring me one from the merry tree,' and away flew the cuckoo.

"'This is the Feast of All Fools, and it ought to be your birthday,' said Scrub. 'Did ever man fling away such an opportunity of getting rich! Much good your merry leaves will do in the midst of rags and poverty!' So he went on, but Spare laughed at him, and answered with quaint old proverbs concerning the cares that come with gold, till Scrub, at length getting angry, vowed his brother was not fit to live with a respectable man; and, taking his lasts, his awls, and his golden leaf, he left the wattle hut, and went to tell the villagers.

"They were astonished at the folly of Spare and charmed with Scrub's good sense, particularly when he showed them the golden leaf, and told that the cuckoo would bring him one every spring. The new cobbler immediately took him into partnership; the greatest people sent him their shoes to mend; Fairfeather smiled graciously upon him, and in the course of that summer they were married, with a grand wedding feast, at which the whole village danced, except Spare, who was not invited, because the bride could not bear his low-mindedness, and his brother thought him a disgrace to the family.

"Indeed, all who heard the story concluded that Spare must be mad, and nobody would associate with him but a lame tinker, a beggar-boy, and a poor woman reputed to be a witch because she was old and ugly. As for Scrub, he established himself with Fairfeather in a cottage close by that of the new cobbler, and quite as fine. There he mended shoes to everybody's satisfaction, had a scarlet coat for holidays, and a fat goose for dinner every wedding-day. Fairfeather, too, had a crimson gown and fine blue ribands; but neither she nor Scrub were content, for to buy this grandeur the golden leaf had to be broken and parted with piece by piece, so the last morsel was gone before the cuckoo came with another.

"Spare lived on in the old hut, and worked in the cabbage garden. (Scrub had got the barley field because he was the eldest.) Every day his coat grew more ragged, and the hut more weatherbeaten; but people remarked that he never looked sad nor sour; and the wonder was, that from the time they began to keep his company, the tinker grew kinder to the poor ass with which he traveled the country, the beggar-boy kept out of mischief, and the old woman was never cross to her cat or angry with the children.

"Every first of April the cuckoo came tapping at their doors with the golden leaf to Scrub and the green to Spare. Fairfeather would have entertained him nobly with wheaten bread and honey, for she had some notion of persuading him to bring two gold leaves instead of one; but the cuckoo flew away to eat barley bread with Spare, saying he was not fit company for fine people, and liked the old hut where he slept so snugly from Christmas till spring.

"Scrub spent the golden leaves, and Spare kept the merry ones; and I know not how many years passed in this manner, when a certain great lord, who owned that village, came to the neighborhood. His castle stood on the moor. It was ancient and strong, with high towers and a deep moat. All the country, as far as one could see from the highest turret, belonged to its lord; but he had not been there for twenty years, and would not have come then, only he was melancholy. The cause of his grief was that he had been prime-minister at court, and in high favor, till somebody told the crown-prince that he had spoken disrespectfully concerning the turning out of his royal highness's toes, and the king that he did not lay on taxes enough, whereon the north country lord was turned out of office, and banished to his own estate. There he lived for some weeks in very bad temper. The servants said nothing would please him, and the villagers put on their worst clothes lest he should raise their rents; but one day in the harvest time his lordship chanced to meet Spare gathering water cresses at a meadow stream, and fell into talk with the cobbler.

"How it was nobody could tell, but from the hour of that discourse the great lord cast away his melancholy: he forgot his lost office and his court enemies, the king's taxes and the crown-prince's toes, and went about with a noble train hunting, fishing, and making merry in his hall, where all travelers were entertained and all the poor were welcome. This strange story spread through the north country, and great company came to the cobbler's hut—rich men who had lost their money, poor men who had lost their friends, beauties who had grown old, wits who had gone out of fashion, all came to talk with Spare, and whatever their troubles had been, all went home merry. The rich gave him presents, the poor gave him thanks. Spare's coat ceased to be ragged, he had bacon with his cabbage, and the villagers began to think there was some sense in him.

"By this time his fame had reached the capital city, and even the court. There were a great many discontented people there besides the king, who had lately fallen into ill-humor because a neighboring princess, with seven islands for her dowry, would not marry his eldest son. So a royal messenger was sent to Spare, with a velvet mantle, a diamond ring, and a command that he should repair to court immediately.

"'To-morrow is the first of April,' said Spare, 'and I will go with you two hours after sunrise.'

"The messenger lodged all night at the castle, and the cuckoo came at sunrise with the merry leaf.

"'Court is a fine place,' he said when the cobbler told him he was going; 'but I cannot come there, they would lay snares and catch me; so be careful of the leaves I have brought you, and give me a farewell slice of barley bread.'"

"Spare was sorry to part with the cuckoo, little as he had of his company; but he gave him a slice which would have broken Scrub's heart in former times, it was so thick and large; and having sewed up the leaves in the lining of his leather doublet, he set out with the messenger on his way to court.

"His coming caused great surprise there. Everybody wondered what the king could see in such a common-looking man; but scarce had his majesty conversed with him half an hour, when the princess and her seven islands were forgotten, and orders given that a feast for all comers should be spread in the banquet hall. The princes of the blood, the great lords and ladies, ministers of state, and judges of the land, after that discoursed with Spare, and the more they talked the lighter grew their hearts, so that such changes had never been seen at court. The lords forgot their spites and the ladies their envies, the princes and ministers made friends among themselves, and the judges showed no favor.

"As for Spare, he had a Chamber assigned him in the palace, and a seat at the king's table; one sent him rich robes and another costly jewels; but in the midst of all his grandeur he still wore the leathern doublet, which the palace servants thought remarkably mean. One day the king's attention being drawn to it by the chief page, his majesty inquired why Spare didn't give it to a beggar. But the cobbler answered:

"'High and mighty monarch, this doublet was with me before silk and velvet came—I find it easier to wear than the court cut; moreover, it serves to keep me humble, by recalling the days when it was my holiday garment.'

"The king thought this a wise speech, and commanded that no one should find fault with the leathern doublet. So things went, till tidings of his brother's good fortune reached Scrub in the moorland cottage on another first of April, when the cuckoo came with two golden leaves, because he had none to carry for Spare.

"'Think of that!' said Fairfeather. 'Here we are spending our lives in this humdrum place, and Spare making his fortune at court with two or three paltry green leaves! What would they say to our golden ones? Let us pack up and make our way to the king's palace; I'm sure he will make you a lord and me a lady of honor, not to speak of all the fine clothes and presents we shall have.'

"Scrub thought this excellent reasoning, and their packing up began: but it was soon found that the cottage contained few things fit for carrying to court. Fairfeather could not think of her wooden bowls, spoons, and trenchers being seen there. Scrub considered his lasts and awls better left behind, as without them, he concluded, no one would suspect him of being a cobbler. So putting on their holiday clothes, Fairfeather took her looking-glass and Scrub his drinking horn, which happened to have a very thin rim of silver, and each carrying a golden leaf carefully wrapped up that none might see it till they reached the palace, the pair set out in great expectation.

"How far Scrub and Fairfeather journeyed I cannot say, but when the sun was high and warm at noon, they came into a wood both tired and hungry.

"'If I had known it was so far to court,' said Scrub, 'I would have brought the end of that barley loaf which we left in the cupboard.'

"'Husband,' said Fairfeather, 'you shouldn't have such mean thoughts: how could one eat barley bread on the way to a palace? Let us rest ourselves under this tree, and look at our golden leaves to see if they are safe.' In looking at the leaves, and talking of their fine prospects, Scrub and Fairfeather did not perceive that a very thin old woman had slipped from behind the tree, with a long staff in her hand and a great wallet by her side.

"'Noble lord and lady,' she said, 'for I know ye are such by your voices, though my eyes are dim and my hearing none of the sharpest, will ye condescend to tell me where I may find some water to mix a bottle of mead which I carry in my wallet, because it is too strong for me?'

"As the old woman spoke, she pulled out a large wooden bottle such as shepherds used in the ancient times, corked with leaves rolled together, and having a small wooden cup hanging from its handle.

"'Perhaps ye will do me the favor to taste,' she said. 'It is only made of the best honey. I have also cream cheese, and a wheaten loaf here, if such honorable persons as you would eat the like.'

"Scrub and Fairfeather became very condescending after this speech. They were now sure that there must be some appearance of nobility about them; besides, they were very hungry, and having hastily wrapped up the golden leaves, they assured the old woman they were not at all proud, notwithstanding the lands and castles they had left behind them in the north country, and would willingly help to lighten the wallet. The old woman could scarcely be persuaded to sit down for pure humility, but at length she did, and before the wallet was half empty, Scrub and Fairfeather firmly believed that there must be something remarkably noble-looking about them. This was not entirely owing to her ingenious discourse. The old woman was a wood-witch; her name was Buttertongue; and all her time was spent in making mead, which, being boiled with curious herbs and spells, had the power of making all who drank it fall asleep and dream with their eyes open. She had two dwarfs of sons; one was named Spy, and the other Pounce. Wherever their mother went they were not far behind; and whoever tasted her mead was sure to be robbed by the dwarfs.

"Scrub and Fairfeather sat leaning against the old tree. The cobbler had a lump of cheese in his hand; his wife held fast a hunk of bread. Their eyes and mouths were both open, but they were dreaming of great grandeur at court, when the old woman raised her shrill voice —

"'What ho, my sons! come here and carry home the harvest.'

"No sooner had she spoken, than the two little dwarfs darted out of the neighboring thicket.

"'Idle boys!' cried the mother, 'what have ye done to-day to help our living?'

"'I have been to the city,' said Spy, 'and could see nothing. These are hard times for us—everybody minds their business so contentedly since that cobbler came; but here is a leathern doublet which his page threw out of the window; it's of no use, but I brought it to let you see I was not idle.' And he tossed down Spare's doublet, with the merry leaves in it, which he had carried like a bundle on his little back.

"To explain how Spy came by it, I must tell you that the forest was not far from the great city where Spare lived in such esteem. All things had gone well with the cobbler till the king thought that it was quite unbecoming to see such a worthy man without a servant. His majesty, therefore, to let all men understand his royal favor toward Spare, appointed one of his own pages to wait upon him. The name of this youth was Tinseltoes, and, though he was the seventh of the king's pages, nobody in all the court had grander notions. Nothing could please him that had not gold or silver about it, and his grandmother feared he would hang himself for being appointed page to a cobbler. As for Spare, if anything could have troubled him, this token of his majesty's kindness would have done it.

"The honest man had been so used to serve himself that the page was always in the way, but his merry leaves came to his assistance; and, to the great surprise of his grandmother, Tinseltoes took wonderfully to the new service. Some said it was because Spare gave him nothing to do but play at bowls all day on the palace-green. Yet one thing grieved the heart of Tinseltoes, and that was his master's leathern doublet, but for it he was persuaded people would never remember that Spare had been a cobbler, and the page took a great deal of pains to let him see how unfashionable it was at court; but Spare answered Tinseltoes as he had done the king, and at last, finding nothing better would do, the page got up one fine morning earlier than his master, and tossed the leathern doublet out of the back window into a certain lane where Spy found it, and brought it to his mother.

"'That nasty thing!' said the old woman; 'where is the good in it?'

"By this time, Pounce had taken everything of value from Scrub and Fairfeather — the looking-glass, the silver-rimmed horn, the husband's scarlet coat, the wife's gay mantle, and, above all, the golden leaves, which so rejoiced old Buttertongue and her sons, that they threw the leathern doublet over the sleeping cobbler for a jest, and went off to their hut in the heart of the forest.

"The sun was going down when Scrub and Fairfeather awoke from dreaming that they had been made a lord and a lady, and sat clothed in silk and velvet, feasting with the king in his palace-hall. It was a great disappointment to find their golden leaves and all their best things gone. Scrub tore his hair, and vowed to take the old woman's life, while Fairfeather lamented sore; but Scrub, feeling cold for want of his coat, put on the leathern doublet without asking or caring whence it came.

"Scarcely was it buttoned on when a change came over him; he addressed such merry discourse to Fairfeather, that, instead of lamentations, she made the wood ring with laughter. Both busied themselves in getting up a hut of boughs, in which Scrub kindled a fire with a flint and steel, which, together with his pipe, he had brought unknown to Fairfeather, who had told him the like was never heard of at court. Then they found a pheasant's nest at the root of an old oak, made a meal of roasted eggs, and went to sleep on a heap of long green grass which they had gathered, with nightingales singing all night long in the old trees about them. So it happened that Scrub and Fairfeather stayed day after day in the forest, making their hut larger and more comfortable against the winter, living on wild birds' eggs and berries, and never thinking of their lost golden leaves, or their journey to court.

"In the meantime Spare had got up and missed his doublet. Tinseltoes, of course, said he knew nothing about it. The whole palace was searched, and every servant questioned, till all the court wondered why such a fuss was made about an old leathern doublet. That very day things came back to their old fashion. Quarrels began among the lords, and jealousies among the ladies. The king said his subjects did not pay him half enough taxes, the queen wanted more jewels, the servants took to their old bickerings and got up some new ones. Spare found himself getting wonderfully dull, and very much out of place: nobles began to ask what business a cobbler had at the king's table, and his majesty ordered the palace chronicles to be searched for a precedent. The cobbler was too wise to tell all he had lost with that doublet, but being by this time somewhat familiar with court customs, he proclaimed a reward of fifty gold pieces to any who would bring him news concerning it.

"Scarcely was this made known in the city, when the gates and outer courts of the palace were filled by men, women, and children, some bringing leathern doublets of every cut and color; some with tales of what they had heard and seen in their walks about the neighborhood; and so much news concerning all sorts of great people came out of these stories, that lords and ladies ran to the king with complaints of Spare as a speaker of slander; and his majesty, being now satisfied that there was no example in all the palace records of such a retainer, issued a decree banishing the cobbler for ever from court, and confiscating all his goods in favor of Tinseltoes.

"That royal edict was scarcely published before the page was in full possession of his rich chamber, his costly garments, and all the presents the courtiers had given him; while Spare, having no longer the fifty pieces of gold to give, was glad to make his escape out of the back window, for fear of the nobles, who vowed to be revenged on him, and the crowd, who were prepared to stone him for cheating them about his doublet.

"The window from which Spare let himself down with a strong rope, was that from which Tinseltoes had tossed the doublet, and as the cobbler came down late in the twilight, a poor woodman, with a heavy load of fagots, stopped and stared at him in great astonishment.

"'What's the matter, friend?' said Spare. 'Did you never see a man coming down from a back window before?'

"'Why,' said the woodman, 'the last morning I passed here a leathern doublet came out of that very window, and I'll be bound you are the owner of it.'

"'That I am, friend,' said the cobbler. 'Can you tell me which way that doublet went?'

"'As I walked on,' said the woodman, 'a dwarf, called Spy, bundled it up and ran off to his mother in the forest.'

"'Honest friend,' said Spare, taking off the last of his fine clothes (a grass-green mantle edged with gold), I'll give you this if you will follow the dwarf, and bring me back my doublet.'

"'It would not be good to carry fagots in,' said the woodman. 'But if you want back your doublet, the road to the forest lies at the end of this lane,' and he trudged away.

"Determined to find his doublet, and sure that neither crowd nor courtiers could catch him in the forest, Spare went on his way, and was soon among the tall trees; but neither hut nor dwarf could he see. Moreover, the night came on; the wood was dark and tangled, but here and there the moon shone through its alleys, the great owls flitted about, and the nightingales sang. So he went on, hoping to find some place of shelter. At last the red light of a fire, gleaming through a thicket, led him to the door of a low hut. It stood half open, as if there was nothing to fear, and within he saw his brother Scrub snoring loudly on a bed of grass, at the foot of which lay his own leathern doublet; while Fairfeather, in a kirtle made of plaited rushes, sat roasting pheasants' eggs by the fire.

"'Good evening, mistress,' said Spare, stepping in.

"The blaze shone on him, but so changed was her brother-in-law with his court-life, that Fairfeather did not know him, and she answered far more courteously than was her wont.

"'Good evening, master. Whence come ye so late? but speak low, for my good man has sorely tired himself cleaving wood, and is taking a sleep, as you see, before supper!'

"'A good rest to him,' said Spare, perceiving he was not known. 'I come from the court for a day's hunting, and have lost my way in the forest.'

"'Sit down and have a share of our supper,' said Fairfeather, 'I will put some more eggs in the ashes; and tell me the news of court—I used to think of it long ago when I was young and foolish.'

"'Did you never go there?' said the cobbler. 'So fair a dame as you would make the ladies marvel.'

"'You are pleased to flatter,' said Fairfeather; 'but my husband has a brother there, and we left our moorland village to try our fortune also. An old woman enticed us with fair words and strong drink at the entrance of this forest, where we fell asleep and dreamt of great things; but when we woke, everything had been robbed from us—my looking-glass, my scarlet cloak, my husband's Sunday coat; and, in place of all, the robbers left him that old leathern doublet, which he has worn ever since, and never was so merry in all his life, though we live in this poor hut.'

"'It is a shabby doublet, that,' said Spare, taking up the garment, and seeing that it was his own, for the merry leaves were still sewed in its lining. 'It would be good for hunting in, however—your husband would be glad to part with it, I dare say, in exchange for this handsome cloak;' and he pulled off the green mantle and buttoned on the doublet, much to Fairfeather's delight, who ran and shook Scrub, crying—"'Husband! husband! rise and see what a good bargain I have made.'

"Scrub gave one closing snore, and muttered something about the root being hard; but he rubbed his eyes, gazed up at his brother, and said—

"'Spare, is that really you? How did you like the court, and have you made your fortune?'

"'That I have, brother,' said Spare, 'in getting back my own good leathern doublet. Come, let us eat eggs, and rest ourselves here this night. In the morning we will return to our own old hut, at the end of the moorland village where the Christmas Cuckoo will come and bring us leaves.'

"Scrub and Fairfeather agreed. So in the morning they all returned, and found the old hut little the worse for wear and weather. The neighbors came about them to ask the news of court, and see if they had made their fortune. Everybody was astonished to find the three poorer than ever, but somehow they liked to go back to the hut. Spare brought out the lasts and awls he had hidden in a corner; Scrub and he began their old trade, and the whole north country found out that there never were such cobblers.

"They mended the shoes of lords and ladies as well as the common people; everybody was satisfied. Their custom increased from day to day, and all that were disappointed, discontented, or unlucky, came to the hut as in old times, before Spare went to court.

"The rich brought them presents, the poor did them service. The hut itself changed, no one knew how. Flowering honeysuckle grew over its roof; red and white roses grew thick about its door. Moreover, the Christmas Cuckoo always came on the first of April, bringing three leaves of the merry tree — for Scrub and Fairfeather would have no more golden ones. So it was with them when I last heard the news of the north country."

THE EMPEROR'S VISION

IT happened at the time when Augustus was Emperor in Rome and Herod was King in Jerusalem.

It was then that a very great and holy night sank down over the earth. It was the darkest night that any one had ever seen. One could have believed that the whole earth had fallen into a cellar-vault. It was impossible to distinguish water from land, and one could not find one's way on the most familiar road. And it couldn't be otherwise, for not a ray of light came from heaven. All the stars stayed at home in their own houses, and the fair moon held her face averted.

The silence and the stillness were as profound as the darkness. The rivers stood still in their courses, the wind did not stir, and even the aspen leaves had ceased to quiver. Had any one walked along the sea-shore, he would have found that the waves no longer dashed upon the sands; and had one wandered in the desert, the sand would not have crunched under one's feet. Everything was as motionless as if turned to stone, so as not to disturb the holy night. The grass was afraid to grow, the dew could not fall, and the flowers dared not exhale their perfume.

On this night the wild beasts did not seek their prey, the serpents did not sting, and the dogs did not bark. And what was even more glorious, inanimate things would have been unwilling to disturb the night's sanctity, by lending themselves to an evil deed. No false key could have picked a lock, and no knife could possibly have drawn a drop of blood.

In Rome, during this very night, a small company of people came from the Emperor's palace at the Palatine and took the path across the Forum which led to the Capitol. During the day just ended the Senators had asked the Emperor if he had any objections to their erecting a temple to him on Rome's sacred hill. But Augustus had not immediately given his consent. He did not know if it would be agreeable to the gods that he should own a temple next to theirs, and he had replied that first he wished to ascertain their will in the matter by offering a nocturnal sacrifice to his genius. It was he who, accompanied by a few trusted friends, was on his way to perform this sacrifice.

Augustus let them carry him in his litter, for he was old, and it was an effort for him to climb the long stairs leading to the Capitol. He himself held the cage with the doves for the sacrifice. No priests or soldiers or senators accompanied him, only his nearest friends. Torch-bearers walked in front of him in order to light the way in the night darkness and behind him followed the slaves, who carried the tripod, the knives, the charcoal, the sacred fire, and all the other things needed for the sacrifice.

On the way the Emperor chatted gayly with his faithful followers, and therefore none of them noticed the infinite silence and stillness of the night. Only when they had reached the highest point of the Capitol Hill and the vacant spot upon which they contemplated erecting the temple, did it dawn upon them that something unusual was taking place.

It could not be a night like all others, for up on the very edge of the cliff they saw the most remarkable being! At first they thought it was an old, distorted olive-trunk; later they imagined that an ancient stone figure from the temple of Jupiter had wandered out on the cliff. Finally it was apparent to them that it could be only the old sibyl.

Anything so aged, so weather-beaten, and so giantlike in stature they had never seen. This old woman was awe-inspiring! If the Emperor had not been present, they would all have fled to their homes.

"It is she," they whispered to each other, "who has lived as many years as there are sand-grains on her native shores. Why has she come out from her cave just to-night? What does she foretell for the Emperor and the Empire—she, who writes her prophecies on the leaves of the trees and knows that the wind will carry the words of the oracle to the person for whom they are intended?"

They were so terrified that they would have dropped on their knees with their foreheads pressed against the earth, had the sibyl stirred. But she sat as still as though she were lifeless. Crouching upon the outermost edge of the cliff, and shading her eyes with her hand, she peered out into the night. She sat there as if she had gone up on the hill that she might see more clearly something that was happening far away. She could see things on a night like this!

At that moment the Emperor and all his retinue, marked how profound the darkness was. None of them could see a hand's breadth in front of him. And what stillness! What silence! Not even the Tiber's hollow murmur could they hear. The air seemed to suffocate them, cold sweat broke out on their foreheads, and their hands were numb and powerless. They feared that some dreadful disaster was impending.

But no one cared to show that he was afraid, and every one told the Emperor that this was a good omen. All Nature held its breath to greet a new god.

They counseled Augustus to hurry with the sacrifice, and said that the old sibyl had evidently come out of her cave to greet his genius.

But the truth was that the old sibyl was so absorbed in a vision that she did not even know that Augustus had come up to the Capitol. She was transported in spirit to a far-distant land, where she imagined that she was wandering over a great plain. In the darkness she stubbed her foot continually against something, which she believed to be grass-tufts. She stooped down and felt with her hand. No, it was not grass, but sheep. She was walking between great sleeping flocks of sheep.

Then she noticed the shepherds' fire. It burned in the middle of the field, and she groped her way to it. The shepherds lay asleep by the fire, and beside them were the long, spiked staves with which they defended their flocks from wild beasts. But the little animals with the glittering eyes and the bushy tails that stole up to the fire, were they not jackals? And yet the shepherds did not fling their staves at them, the dogs continued to sleep, the sheep did not flee, and the wild animals lay down to rest beside the human beings.

This the sibyl saw, but she knew nothing of what was being enacted on the hill back of her. She did not know that there they were raising an altar, lighting charcoal and strewing incense, and that the Emperor took one of the doves from the cage to sacrifice it. But his hands were so benumbed that he could not hold the bird. With one stroke of the wing, it freed itself and disappeared in the night darkness.

When this happened, the courtiers glanced suspiciously at the old sibyl. They believed that it was she who caused the misfortune.

Could they know that all the while the sibyl thought herself standing beside the shepherds' fire, and that she listened to a faint sound which came trembling through the dead-still night? She heard it long before she marked that it did not come from earth, but from the sky. At last she raised her head; then she saw light, shimmering forms glide forward in the darkness. They were little flocks of angels, who, singing joyously, and apparently searching, flew back and forth above the wide plain.

While the sibyl was listening to the angel-song, the Emperor was making preparations for a new sacrifice. He washed his hands, cleansed the altar, and took up the other dove. And, although he exerted his full strength to hold it fast, the dove's slippery body slid from his hand, and the bird swung itself up into the impenetrable night.

The Emperor was appalled! He fell upon his knees and prayed to his genius. He implored him for strength to avert the disasters which this night seemed to foreshadow.

Nor did the sibyl hear any of this either. She was listening with her whole soul to the angel-song, which grew louder and louder. At last it became so powerful that it wakened the shepherds. They raised themselves on their elbows and saw shining hosts of silver-white angels move in the darkness in long swaying lines, like migratory birds. Some held lutes and cymbals in their hands; others held zithers and harps, and their song rang out as merry as child-laughter, and as carefree as the lark's thrill. When the shepherds heard this, they rose up to go to the mountain city, where they lived, to tell of the miracle.

They groped their way forward on a narrow, winding path, and the sibyl followed them. Suddenly it grew light up there on the mountain: a big, clear star kindled right over it, and the city on the mountain summit glittered like silver in the starlight. All the fluttering angel throngs hastened thither, shouting for joy, and the shepherds hurried so that they almost ran. When they reached the city, they found that the angels had assembled over a low stable near the city gate. It was a wretched structure, with a roof of straw and the naked cliff for a back wall. Over it hung the Star, and hither flocked more and more angels. Some seated themselves on the straw roof or alighted upon the steep mountain-wall back of the house; others, again, held themselves in the air on outspread wings, and hovered over it. High, high up, the air was illuminated by the shining wings.

The instant the Star kindled over the mountain city, all Nature awoke, and the men who stood upon Capitol Hill could not help seeing it. They felt fresh, but caressing winds which traveled through space; delicious perfumes streamed up about them; trees swayed; the Tiber began to murmur; the stars twinkled, and suddenly the moon stood out in the sky and lit up the world. And out of the clouds the two doves came circling down and lighted upon the Emperor's shoulders.

When this miracle happened, Augustus rose, proud and happy, but his friends and his slaves fell on their knees.

"Hail, Cæsar!" they cried. "Thy genius hath answered thee. Thou art the god who shall be worshiped on Capitol Hill!"

And this cry of homage, which the men in their transport gave as a tribute to the emperor, was so loud that the old sibyl heard it. It waked her from her visions. She rose from her place on the edge of the cliff, and came down among the people. It was as if a dark cloud had arisen from the abyss and rushed down the mountain height. She was terrifying in her extreme age! Coarse hair hung in matted tangles around her head, her joints were enlarged, and the dark skin, hard as the bark of a tree, covered her body with furrow upon furrow.

Potent and awe-inspiring, she advanced toward the Emperor. With one hand she clutched his wrist, with the other she pointed toward the distant East.

"Look!" she commanded, and the Emperor raised his eyes and saw. The vaulted heavens opened before his eyes, and his glance traveled to the

83

distant Orient. He saw a lowly stable behind a steep rock wall, and in the open doorway a few shepherds kneeling. Within the stable he saw a young mother on her knees before a little child, who lay upon a bundle of straw on the floor.

And the sibyl's big, knotty fingers pointed toward the poor babe. "Hail, Cæsar!" cried the sibyl, in a burst of scornful laughter. "There is the god who shall be worshiped on Capitol Hill!"

Then Augustus shrank back from her, as from a maniac. But upon the sibyl fell the mighty spirit of prophecy. Her dim eyes began to burn, her hands were stretched toward heaven, her voice was so changed that it seemed not to be her own, but rang out with such resonance and power that it could have been heard over the whole world. And she uttered words which she appeared to be reading among the stars.

"Upon Capitol Hill shall the Redeemer of the world be worshiped — Christ — but not frail mortals."

When she had said this, she strode past the terror-stricken men, walked slowly down the mountain, and disappeared.

But, on the following day, Augustus strictly forbade the people to raise any temple to him on Capitol Hill. In place of it he built a sanctuary to the new-born GodChild, and called it HEAVEN'S ALTAR — Ara Coeli.

THE VOYAGE OF THE WEE RED CAP

IT was the Eve of St. Stephen, and Teig sat alone by his fire with naught in his cupboard but a pinch of tea and a bare mixing of meal, and a heart inside of him as soft and warm as the ice on the water bucket outside the door. The tuft was near burnt on the hearth—a handful of golden cinders left, just; and Teig took to counting them greedily on his fingers.

"There's one, two, three, an' four an' five," he laughed. "Faith, there be more bits o' real gold hid undther the loose clay in the corner."

It was the truth; and it was the scraping and scrooching for the last piece that had left Teig's cupboard bare of a Christmas dinner.

"Gold is betther nor eatin' an' dthrinkin'. An' if ye have naught to give, there'll be naught asked of ye;" and he laughed again.

He was thinking of the neighbors, and the doles of food and piggins of milk that would pass over their thresholds that night to the vagabonds and paupers who were sure to come begging. And on the heels of that thought followed another: who would be giving old Barney his dinner? Barney lived a stone's throw from Teig, alone, in a wee tumbled-in cabin; and for a score of years past Teig had stood on the doorstep every Christmas Eve, and, making a hollow of his two hands, had called across the road:

"Hey, there, Barney, will ye come over for a sup?" And Barney had reached for his crutches—there being but one leg to him—and had come.

"Faith," said Teig, trying another laugh, "Barney can fast for the once; 'twill be all the same in a month's time." And he fell to thinking of the gold again.

A knock came at the door. Teig pulled himself down in his chair where the shadow would cover him, and held his tongue.

"Teig, Teig!" It was the widow O'Donnelly's voice. "If ye are there, open your door. I have not got the pay for the spriggin' this month, an' the childher are needin' food."

But Teig put the leash on his tongue, and never stirred till he heard the tramp of her feet going on to the next cabin. Then he saw to it that the door was tight-barred. Another knock came, and it was a stranger's voice this time:

"The other cabins are filled; not one but has its hearth crowded; will ye take us in—the two of us? The wind bites mortal sharp, not a morsel o' food have we tasted this day. Masther, will ye take us in?"

But Teig sat on, a-holding his tongue; and the tramp of the strangers' feet passed down the road. Others took their place—small feet, running. It was the miller's wee Cassie, and she called out as she ran by:

"Old Barney's watchin' for ye. Ye'll not be forget-tin' him, will ye, Teig?"

And then the child broke into a song, sweet and clear, as she passed down the road:

"Listen all ye, 'tis the Feast o' St. Stephen,

Mind that ye keep it, this holy even.

Open your door an' greet ye the stranger—

For ye mind that the wee Lord had naught but a manger.

Mhuire as traugh!

"Feed ye the hungry an' rest ye the weary,

This ye must do for the sake of Our Mary.

'Tis well that ye mind—ye who sit by the fire—

That the Lord he was born in a dark and cold byre.

Mhuire as traugh!

Teig put his fingers deep in his ears. "A million murdthering curses on them that won't let me be! Can't a man try to keep what is his without bein' pesthered by them that has only idled an' wasted their days?"

And then a strange thing happened: hundreds and hundreds of wee lights began dancing outside the window, making the room bright; the hands of the clock began chasing each other round the dial, and the bolt of the door drew itself out. Slowly, without a creak or a cringe, the door opened, and in

86

there trooped a crowd of the Good People. Their wee green cloaks were folded close about them, and each carried a rush candle.

Teig was filled with a great wonderment, entirely, when he saw the fairies, but when they saw him they laughed.

"We are takin' the loan o' your cabin this night, Teig," said they. "Ye are the only man hereabout with an empty hearth, an' we're needin' one."

Without saying more, they bustled about the room making ready. They lengthened out the table and spread and set it; more of the Good People trooped in, bringing stools and food and drink. The pipers came last, and they sat themselves around the chimney-piece a-blowing their chanters and trying the drones. The feasting began and the pipers played and never had Teig seen such a sight in his life. Suddenly a wee man sang out:

"Clip, clap, clip, clap, I wish I had my wee red cap!" And out of the air there tumbled the neatest cap Teig ever laid his two eyes on. The wee man clapped it on his head, crying:

"I wish I was in Spain!" and—whist—up the chimney he went, and away out of sight.

It happened just as I am telling it. Another wee man called for his cap, and away he went after the first. And then another and another until the room was empty and Teig sat alone again.

"By my soul," said Teig, "I'd like to thravel that way myself! It's a grand savin' of tickets an' baggage; an' ye get to a place before ye've had time to change your mind. Faith there is no harm done if I thry it."

So he sang the fairies' rime and out of the air dropped a wee cap for him. For a moment the wonder had him, but the next he was clapping the cap on his head and crying:

"Spain!"

Then—whist—up the chimney he went after the fairies, and before he had time to let out his breath he was standing in the middle of Spain, and strangeness all about him.

He was in a great city. The doorways of the houses were hung with flowers and the air was warm and sweet with the smell of them. Torches burned along the streets, sweetmeat-sellers went about crying their wares, and on the steps of the cathedral crouched a crowd of beggars.

"What's the meanin' o' that?" asked Teig of one of the fairies.

"They are waiting for those that are hearing mass. When they come out, they give half of what they have to those that have nothing, so on this night of all the year there shall be no hunger and no cold."

And then far down the street came the sound of a child's voice, singing:

"Listen all ye, 'tis the Feast o' St. Stephen,

Mind that ye keep it, this holy even."

"Curse it!" said Teig; "can a song fly afther ye?" And then he heard the fairies cry "Holland!" and he cried "Holland!" too.

In one leap he was over France, and another over Belgium; and with the third he was standing by long ditches of water frozen fast, and over them glided hundreds upon hundreds of lads and maids. Outside each door stood a wee wooden shoe empty. Teig saw scores of them as he looked down the ditch of a street.

"What is the meanin' o' those shoes?" he asked the fairies.

"Ye poor lad!" answered the wee man next to him; "are ye not knowing anything? This is the Gift Night of the year, when every man gives to his neighbor."

A child came to the window of one of the houses, and in her hand was a lighted candle. She was singing as she put the light down close to the glass, and Teig caught the words:

"Open your door an' greet ye the stranger —

For ye mind that the wee Lord had naught but a manger.

Mhuire as traugh!"

"'Tis the de'il's work!" cried Teig, and he set the red cap more firmly on his head.

"I'm for another country."

I cannot be telling you half the adventures Teig had that night, nor half the sights that he saw. But he passed by fields that held sheaves of grain for the birds and doorsteps that held bowls of porridge for the wee creatures. He saw lighted trees, sparkling and heavy with gifts; and he stood outside the churches and watched the crowds pass in, bearing gifts to the Holy Mother and Child.

At last the fairies straightened their caps and cried, "Now for the great hall in the King of England's palace!"

Whist—and away they went, and Teig after them; and the first thing he knew he was in London, not an arm's length from the King's throne. It was a grander sight than he had seen in any other country. The hall was filled entirely with lords and ladies; and the great doors were open for the poor and the homeless to come in and warm themselves by the King's fire and feast from the King's table. And many a hungry soul did the King serve with his own hands.

Those that had anything to give gave it in return. It might be a bit of music played on a harp or a pipe, or it might be a dance or a song; but more often it was a wish, just, for good luck and safekeeping.

Teig was so taken up with the watching that he never heard the fairies when they wished themselves off; moreover, he never saw the wee girl that was fed, and went laughing away. But he heard a bit of her song as she passed through the door:

"Feed ye the hungry an' rest ye the weary,

This ye must do for the sake of Our Mary."

Then the anger had Teig. "I'll stop your pestherin' tongue, once an' for all time!" and, catching the cap from his head, he threw it after her.

No sooner was the cap gone than every soul in the hall saw him. The next moment they were about him, catching at his coat and crying:

"Where is he from, what does he here? Bring him before the King!" And Teig was dragged along by a hundred hands to the throne where the King sat.

"He was stealing food," cried one.

"He was robbing the King's jewels," cried another.

"He looks evil," cried a third. "Kill him!"

And in a moment all the voices took it up and the hall rang with: "Aye, kill him, kill him!"

Teig's legs took to trembling, and fear put the leash on his tongue; but after a long silence he managed to whisper:

"I have done evil to no one — no one!"

"Maybe," said the King; "but have ye done good? Come, tell us, have ye given aught to any one this night? If ye have, we will pardon ye."

Not a word could Teig say — fear tightened the leash — for he was knowing full well there was no good to him that night.

"Then ye must die," said the King. "Will ye try hanging or beheading?"

"Hanging, please, your Majesty," said Teig.

The guards came rushing up and carried him off. But as he was crossing the threshold of the hall a thought sprang at him and held him.

"Your Majesty," he called after him, "will ye grant me a last request?"

"I will," said the King.

"Thank ye. There's a wee red cap that I'm mortal fond of, and I lost it a while ago; if I could be hung with it on, I would hang a deal more comfortable."

The cap was found and brought to Teig.

"Clip, clap, clip, clap, for my wee red cap, I wish I was home," he sang.

Up and over the heads of the dumfounded guard he flew, and — whist — and away out of sight. When he opened his eyes again, he was sitting close by his own hearth, with the fire burnt low. The hands of the clock were still, the bolt was fixed firm in the door. The fairies' lights were gone, and the only bright thing was the candle burning in old Barney's cabin across the road.

A running of feet sounded outside, and then the snatch of a song:

"'Tis well that ye mind—ye who sit by the fire—

That the Lord he was born in a dark and cold byre.

Mhuire as traugh!"

"Wait ye, whoever ye are!" and Teig was away to the corner, digging fast at the loose clay, as a terrier digs at a bone. He filled his hands full of the shining gold, then hurried to the door, unbarring it.

The miller's wee Cassie stood there, peering at him out of the darkness.

"Take those to the widow O'Donnelly, do ye hear? And take the rest to the store. Ye tell Jamie to bring up all that he has that is eatable an' dhrinkable; and to the neighbors ye say, 'Teig's keepin' the feast this night.' Hurry now!"

Teig stopped a moment on the threshold until the tramp of her feet had died away; then he made a hollow of his two hands and called across the road:

"Hey there, Barney, will ye come over for a sup?"

GREEK LEGENDS
THE CURSE OF ECHO

IN the flowery groves of Helicon, Echo was once a fair nymph who, hand in hand with her sisters, sported along the green lawns and by the side of the mountain-streams. Among them all her feet were the lightest and her laugh the merriest, and in the telling of tales not one of them could touch her. So if ever any among them were plotting mischief in their hearts, they would say to her:

"Echo, thou weaver of words, go thou and sit beside Hera in her bower, and beguile her with a tale that she come not forth and find us. See thou make it a long one, Echo, and we will give thee a garland to twine in thy hair."

And Echo would laugh a gay laugh, which rang through the grove.

"What will you do when she tires of my tales?" she asked.

"When that time comes we shall see," said they.

So with another laugh she would trip away and cast herself on the grass at Hera's feet. When Hera looked upon Echo her stern brow would relax, and she would smile upon her and stroke her hair.

"What hast thou come for now, thou sprite?" she would ask.

"I had a great longing to talk with thee, great Hera," she would answer, "and I have a tale — a wondrous new tale — to tell thee."

"Thy tales are as many as the risings of the sun, Echo, and each one of them as long as an old man's beard."

"The day is yet young, mother," she would say, "and the tales I have told thee before are as mud which is trampled underfoot by the side of the one I shall tell thee now."

"Go to, then," said Hera, "and if it pleases me I will listen to the end."

So Echo would sit upon the grass at Hera's feet, and with her eyes fixed upon her face she would tell her tale. She had the gift of words, and, moreover, she had seen and heard many strange things which she alone could tell of. These she would weave into romances, adding to them as best pleased her, or taking from them at will; for the best of tale-tellers are those who can lie, but who mingle in with their lies some grains of truth which they have picked from their own experience. And Hera would forget her watchfulness and her jealousies, and listen entranced, while the magic of Echo's words made each scene live before her eyes. Meanwhile the nymphs would sport to their hearts' content and never fear her anger.

But at last came the black day of reckoning when Hera found out the prank which Echo had played upon her so long, and the fire of her wrath flashed forth like lightning.

"The gift whereby thou hast deceived me shall be thine no more," she cried. "Henceforward thou shalt be dumb till some one else has spoken, and then, even if thou wilt, thou shalt not hold thy tongue, but must needs repeat once more the last words that have been spoken."

"Alas! alas!" cried the nymphs in chorus.

"Alas! alas!" cried Echo after them, and could say no more, though she longed to speak and beg Hera to forgive her. So did it come to pass that she lost her voice, and could only say that which others put in her mouth, whether she wished it or no.

Now, it chanced one day that the young Narcissus strayed away from his companions in the hunt, and when he tried to find them he only wandered further, and lost his way upon the lonely heights of Helicon. He was now in the bloom of his youth, nearing manhood, and fair as a flower in spring, and all who saw him straightway loved him and longed for him. But, though his face was smooth and soft as maiden's, his heart was hard as steel; and while many loved him and sighed for him, they could kindle no answering flame in his breast, but he would spurn them, and treat them with scorn, and go on his way, nothing caring. When he was born, the blind seer Teiresias had prophesied concerning him:

"So long as he sees not himself he shall live and be happy."

And his words came true, for Narcissus cared for neither man nor woman, but only for his own pleasure; and because he was so fair that all who saw him loved him for his beauty, he found it easy to get from them what he would. But he himself knew naught of love, and therefore but little of grief; for love at the best brings joy and sorrow hand in hand, and if unreturned, it brings naught but pain.

Now, when the nymphs saw Narcissus wandering alone through the woods, they, too, loved him for his beauty, and they followed him wherever he went. But because he was a mortal they were shy of him, and would not show themselves, but hid behind the trees and rocks so that he should not see them; and amongst the others Echo followed him, too. At last, when he found he had really wandered astray, he began to shout for one of his companions.

"Ho, there! where art thou?" he cried.

"Where art thou?" answered Echo.

When he heard the voice, he stopped and listened, but he could hear nothing more. Then he called again.

"I am here in the wood—Narcissus."

"In the wood—Narcissus," said she.

"Come hither," he cried.

"Come hither," she answered.

Wondering at the strange voice which answered him, he looked all about, but could see no one.

"Art thou close at hand?" he asked.

"Close at hand," answered Echo.

Wondering the more at seeing no one, he went forward in the direction of the voice. Echo, when she found he was coming towards her, fled further, so that when next he called, her voice sounded far away. But wherever she was, he still followed after her, and she saw that he would not let her escape; for wherever she hid, if he called, she had to answer, and so show him her hiding-place. By now they had come to an open space in the trees, where the green lawn sloped down to a clear pool in the hollow. Here by the margin of the water she stood, with her back to the tall, nodding bulrushes, and as Narcissus came out from the trees she wrung her hands, and the salt tears dropped from her eyes; for she loved him, and longed to speak to him, and yet she could not say a word. When he saw her he stopped.

"Art thou she who calls me?" he asked.

"Who calls me?" she answered.

"I have told thee, Narcissus," he said.

"Narcissus," she cried, and held out her arms to him.

"Who art thou?" he asked.

"Who art thou?" said she.

"Have I not told thee," he said impatiently, "Narcissus?"

"Narcissus," she said again, and still held out her hands beseechingly.

"Tell me," he cried, "who art thou and why dost thou call me?"

"Why dost thou call me?" said she.

At this he grew angry.

"Maiden, whoever thou art, thou hast led me a pretty dance through the woods, and now thou dost nought but mock me."

"Thou dost nought but mock me," said she.

At this he grew yet more angry, and began to abuse her, but every word of abuse that he spoke she hurled back at him again. At last, tired out with his wanderings and with anger, he threw himself on the grass by the pool, and would not look at her nor speak to her again. For a time she stood beside him weeping, and longing to speak to him and explain, but never a word could she utter. So at last in her misery she left him, and went and hid herself behind a rock close by. After a while, when his anger had cooled down somewhat, Narcissus remembered he was very thirsty, and noticing for the first time the clear pool beside him, he bent over the edge of the bank to drink. As he held out his hand to take the water, he saw looking up towards him a face which was the fairest face he had ever looked on, and his heart, which never yet had known what love was, at last was set on fire by the face in the pool. With a sigh he held out both his arms toward it, and the figure also held out two arms to him, and Echo from the rock answered back his sigh. When he saw the figure stretching out towards him and heard the sigh, he thought that his love was returned, and he bent down closer to the water and whispered, "I love thee."

"I love thee," answered Echo from the rock.

At these words he bent down further, and tried to clasp the figure in his arms, but as he did so, it vanished away. The surface of the pool was covered with ripples, and he found he was clasping empty water to his breast. So he drew back and waited awhile, thinking he had been over-hasty. In time, the ripples died away and the face appeared again as clear as before, looking up at him longingly from the water. Once again he bent towards it, and tried to clasp it, and once again it fled from his embrace. Time after time he tried, and always the same thing happened, and at last he gave up in despair, and sat looking down into the water, with the teardrops falling from his eyes; and the figure in the pool wept, too, and looked up at him with a look of longing and despair. The longer he looked, the more fiercely did the flame of love burn in his breast, till at length he could bear it no more, but determined to reach the desire of his heart or die. So for the last time he leaned forward, and when he found that once again he was clasping the empty water, he threw himself from the bank into the pool, thinking that in the depths, at any rate, he would find his love. But he found naught but death among the weeds and stones of the pool, and knew not that it was his own face he loved reflected in the water below him. Thus were the words of the prophet fulfilled, "So long as he sees not himself he shall live and be happy."

Echo, peeping out from the rock, saw all that had happened, and when Narcissus cast himself into the pool she rushed forward, all too late, to stop him. When she found she could not save him, she cast herself on the grass by the pool and wept and wept, till her flesh and her bones wasted away with weeping, and naught but her voice remained and the curse that was on her. So to this day she lives, a formless voice haunting rocks and caves and vaulted halls. Herself no man has seen since the day Narcissus saw her wringing her hands for love of him beside the nodding bulrushes, and no man ever shall see again. But her voice we all have heard repeating our words when we thought that no one was by; and though now she will say whatever we bid her, if once the curse were removed, the cry of her soul would be:

"Narcissus, Narcissus, my love, come back — come back to me!"

By the side of the clear brown pool, on the grass that Echo had watered with her tears, there sprang up a sweet-scented flower, with a pure white face and a crown of gold. And to this day in many a land men call that flower "Narcissus," after the lad who, for love of his own fair face, was drowned in the waters of Helicon.

HOW THE ASS BECAME A MAN AGAIN

ONCE upon a time there lived a young man who would do nothing from morning till night but amuse himself. His parents were dead and had left him plenty of money, but this was fast vanishing, and his friends shook their heads sadly, for when the money was gone they did not see where more was to come from. It was not that Apuleius (for that was the name of the youth) was stupid. He might have been a good soldier, or a scholar, or a worker in gold, if so it had pleased him, but from a child he had refused to do anything useful, and roamed about the city all day long in search of adventures. The only kind of learning to which he paid any heed was magic, and when he was in the house he would spend hours poring over great books of spells.

Fond though he was of sorcery, he was too lazy to leave the town and its pleasures — the chariot-racing, the theater, and the wrestling, and to travel in search of the wizards who were renowned for their skill in the art. However, the time came when, very unwillingly, he was forced to take a journey into Thessaly, to see to the proper working of some silver mines in which he had a share, and Thessaly, as everybody knows, is the home of all magic. So when Apuleius arrived at the town of Hypata, where dwelt the man Milo, overseer of his mines, he was prepared to believe that all he saw was enchanted.

Now, if Thessaly is the country of magic, it is also the country of robbers, and Apuleius soon noticed that everybody he met was in fear of them. Indeed, they made this fear the excuse for all sorts of mean and foolish ways. For instance, Milo, who loved money and could not bear to spend a farthing, refused to have any seats in his house that could be removed, and in consequence there was nothing to sit upon except two marble chairs fixed to the wall. As there was only room in these for one person, the wife of Milo had to retire to her own chamber when the young man entered.

"It was no use," explained Milo, "in laying out money on moveable seats, with robbers about. They would be sure to hear of it and to break into the house."

Unlike his guest, Milo was always occupied in adding to his wealth in one form or another. Sometimes he sent down a train of mules to the sea, and bought merchandise which the ships had carried from Babylon or Egypt, to sell it again at a high price. Then he dealt in sheep and cattle, and when he thought he might do so with safety made false returns of the silver that was dug up from the mines, and kept the difference for himself. But most often he lent large sums at high interest to the young men of the neighborhood, and so cunning was he that, whoever else might be ruined, Milo managed to make large profits.

Apuleius knew very well that his steward was in his way as great a robber as any in Thessaly, but, as usual, he found it too much trouble to look into the matter. So he laughed and jested with the miser, and next morning went out to the public baths and then took a stroll through the city. It was full of statues of the famous men to whom Hypata had given birth; but as Apuleius had made up his mind that nothing in Thessaly could be what it seemed, he supposed that they were living people who had fallen under enchantment, and that the oxen whom he met driven through the streets had once been men and women.

One evening he was returning as usual from a walk when he saw from afar three figures before Milo's house, whom he at once guessed were trying to force an entrance.

"Here is an adventure at last," thought he, and, keeping in the shadow, he stole softly up behind them, and drawing his short sword he stabbed each one to the heart. Then, without waiting to see what more would befall, he left them where they were and entered the house by a door at the back.

He said nothing of what had happened to Milo his host, but the next day, before he had left his bed, a summons was brought him by one of the slaves to appear before the court at noon on a charge of murder. As has been seen, Apuleius was a brave man and did not fear to face three times his number, but his heart quailed at the thought of a public trial. Still, he was wise enough to know that there was no help for it, and at the hour appointed he was in his place.

The first witnesses against him were two women with black veils covering them from head to foot. At the sound of the herald's trumpet, one of the two stepped forward and accused him of compassing the death of her husband. When she had ended her plaint the herald blew another blast, and another veiled woman came forward and charged him with her son's murder. Then the herald inquired if there was notyet a third victim, but was answered that his wound was slight, and that he was able to roam through the city.

After the witnesses had been called, the judge pronounced sentence. Apuleius the murderer was condemned to death, but he must first of all be tortured, so that he might reveal the names of the men who had abetted him. By order of the court, horrible instruments were brought forward which chilled the blood of Apuleius in his veins. But to his surprise, when he looked round to see if none would be his friend, he noticed that every one, from the judge to the herald, was shaking with laughter. His amazement was increased when with a trembling voice one of the women demanded that the bodies should be produced, so that the judge might be induced to feel more pity and to order more tortures. The judge assented to this, and two bodies were carried into court shrouded in wrappings, and the order was given that Apuleius himself should remove the wrappings.

The face of the young man grew white as he heard the words of the judge, for even a hardened criminal cares but little to touch the corpse of a man whom he has murdered. But he dared not disobey, and walked slowly to the place where the dead bodies lay. He shrank for a moment as he took the cloth in his hands, but his guards were behind him, and calling up all his courage, he withdrew it. A shout of laughter pealed out behind him, and to his amazement he saw that his victims of the previous night had been three huge leather bottles and not men at all!

As soon as Apuleius found out the trick that had been played on him he was no less amused than the rest, but in the midst of his mirth a sudden thought struck him.

"How was it you managed to make them alive?" asked he, "for alive they were, and battering themselves against the door of the house."

"Oh, that is simple enough when one has a sorceress for a mistress," answered a damsel, who was standing by. "She burned the hairs of some goats and wove spells over them, so that the animals to whom the hairs and skins had once belonged became endowed with life and tried to enter their former dwelling."

"They may well say that Thessaly is the home of wonders," cried the young man. "But do you think that your mistress would let me see her at work? I would pay her well—and you also," he added.

"It might be managed perhaps, without her knowledge," answered Fotis, for such was the girl's name; "but you must hold yourself in readiness after nightfall, for I cannot tell what evening she may choose to cast off her own shape."

Apuleius promised readily that he would not stir out after sunset, and the damsel went her way.

That very evening, Hesperus had scarcely risen from his bed when Fotis knocked at the door of the house.

"Come hither, and quickly," she said; and without stopping to question her Apuleius hastened by her side to the dwelling of the witch Pamphile. Entering softly, they crept along a dark passage, where they could peep through a crack in the wall and see Pamphile at work. She was in the act of rubbing her body with essences from a long row of bottles which stood in a cupboard in the wall, chanting to herself spells as she did so. Slowly, feathers began to sprout from her head to her feet. Her arms vanished, her nails became claws, her eyes grew round and her nose hooked, and a little brown owl flew out of the window.

"Well, are you satisfied?" asked Fotis, but Apuleius shook his head.

"Not yet," he answered. "I want to know how she transforms herself into a woman again."

"That is quite easy, you may be sure," replied Fotis. "My mistress never runs any risks. A cup of water from a spring, with some laurel leaves and anise floating in it, is all that she needs. I have seen her do it a thousand times."

"Turn me into a nightingale, then, and I will give you five hundred sesterces," cried Apuleius eagerly; and Fotis, tempted by the thought of so much money, agreed to do what he wished.

But either Fotis was not so skilful as she thought herself, or in her hurry she neglected to observe that the bird bottles were all on one shelf, and the beast bottles on another, for when she had rubbed the ointment over the young man's chest something fearful happened. Instead of his arms disappearing, they stretched downwards; his back became bent, his face long and narrow, while a browny-gray fur covered his body. Apuleius had been changed, not into a nightingale, but into an ass!

A loud scream broke from Fotis when she saw what she had done, and Apuleius, glancing at a polished mirror from Corinth which hung on the walls, beheld with horror the fate that had overtaken him.

"Quick, quick! fetch the water, and I will seek for the laurels and anise," he cried. "I do not want to be an ass at all; my arms and back are aching already, and if I am not swiftly restored to my own shape I shall not be able to overthrow the champion in the wrestling match to-morrow."

So Fotis ran out to draw the water from the spring, while Apuleius opened some boxes with his teeth, and soon found the anise and laurels. But alas! Fotis had deceived herself. The charm which was meant for a bird would not work with a beast, and, what was worse, when Apuleius tried to speak to her and beg her to try something else, he found he could only bray!

In despair the girl took down the book of spells, and began to turn over the pages; while the ass, who was still a man in all but his outward form, glanced eagerly down them also. At length he gave a loud bray of satisfaction, and rubbed his nose on a part of the long scroll.

"Of course, I remember now," cried Fotis with delight. "What a comfort that nothing more is needed to restore you to your proper shape than a handful of rose leaves!"

The mind of Apuleius was now quite easy, but his spirits fell again when Fotis reminded him that he could no longer expect to be received by his friends, but must lie in the stable of Milo, with his own horse, and be tended, if he was tended at all, by his own servant.

"However, it will not be for long," she added consolingly. "In the corner of the stable is a little shrine to the goddess of horses, and every day fresh roses are placed before it. Before the sun sets to-morrow you will be yourself again."

Slowly and shyly Apuleius slunk along lonely paths till he came to the stable of Milo. The door was open, but, as he entered, his horse, who was fastened with a sliding cord, kicked wildly at him, and caught him right on the shoulder. But before the horse could deal another blow Apuleius had sprung hastily on one side, and had hidden himself in a dark corner, where he slept soundly.

The moon was shining brightly when he awoke, and looking round, he saw, as Fotis had told him, the shrine of Hippone, with a branch of sweet-smelling pink roses lying before it. It was rather high up, he thought, but, when he reared himself on his hind legs, he would surely be tall enough to reach it. So up he got, and trod softly over the straw, till he drew near the shrine, when with a violent effort he threw up his forelegs into the air. Yes! it was all right, his nose was quite near the roses; but just as he opened his mouth his balance gave way, and his front feet came heavily on the floor.

The noise brought the man, who was sleeping in another part of the stable.

"Oh, I see what you are at, you ugly beast," cried he; "would you eat roses that I put there for the goddess? I don't know who may be your master, or how you got here, but I will take care that you do no more mischief." So saying, he struck the ass several times with his fists, and then, putting a rope round his neck, tied him up in another part of the stable.

Now it happened that an hour or two later some of the most desperate robbers in all Thessaly broke into the house of Milo, and, unheard by any one, took all the bags of money that the miser had concealed under some loose stones in his cellar. It was clear that they could not carry away such heavy plunder without risk of the crime being discovered, but they managed to get it quietly as far as the stable, where they gave the horse some apples to put it in a good temper, while they thrust a turnip into the mouth of Apuleius, who did not like it at all. Then they led out both the animals, and placed the sacks of money on their backs, after which they all set out for the robbers' cave in the side of the mountain. As this, however, was some distance off, it took them many hours to reach it, and on the way they passed through a large deserted garden, where rose bushes of all sorts grew like weeds. The pulse of Apuleius bounded at the sight, and he had already stretched out his nose towards them, when he suddenly remembered that if he should turn into a man in his present company he would probably be murdered by the robbers. With a great effort, he left the roses alone, and tramped steadily on his way.

It were long indeed to tell the adventures of Apuleius and the number of masters whom he served. After some time he was captured by a soldier, and by him sold to two brothers, one a cook and the other a maker of pastry, who were attached to the service of a rich man who lived in the country. This man did not allow any of his slaves to dwell in his house, except those who attended on him personally, and these two brothers lived in a tent on the other side of the garden, and the ass was given to them to send to and fro with savory dishes in his panniers.

The cook and his brother were both careful men, and always had a great store of pastry and sweet things on their shelves, so that none might be lacking if their lord should command them. When they had done their work they placed water and food for their donkey in a little shed which opened on to the tent, then, fastening the door so that no one could enter, they went out to enjoy the evening air.

On their return, it struck them that the tent looked unusually bare, and at length they perceived that this was because every morsel of pastry and sweets on the shelves had disappeared, and nothing was left of them, not so much as a crumb. There was no room for a thief to hide, so the two brothers supposed that, impossible it seemed, he must not only have got in but out by the door, and, as their master might send for a tray of cakes at any moment, there was no help for it but to make a fresh supply. And so they did, and it took them more than half the night to do it.

The next evening the same thing happened again; and the next, and the next, and the next.

Then, by accident, the cook went into the shed where the ass lay, and discovered a heap of corn and hay that reached nearly to the roof.

"Ah, you rascal!" he exclaimed, bursting out laughing as he spoke. "So it is you who have cost us our sleep! Well, well, I dare say I should have done the same myself, for cakes and sweets are certainly nicer than corn and hay." And the donkey brayed in answer, and winked an eye at him, and, more amused than before, the man went away to tell his brother.

Of course it was not long before the story reached the ears of their master, who instantly sent to buy the donkey, and bade one of his servants, who had a taste for such things, teach him fresh tricks. This the man was ready enough to do, for the fame of this wonderful creature soon spread far and wide, and the citizens of the town thronged the doors of his stable. And while the servant reaped much gold by making the ass display his accomplishments, the master gained many friends among the people, and was soon made chief ruler.

For five years Apuleius stayed in the house of Thyasus, and ate as many sweet cakes as he chose; and if he wanted more than were given him he wandered down to the tent of his old masters, and swept the shelves bare as of yore. At the end of the five years Thyasus proclaimed that a great feast would be held in his garden, after which plays would be acted, and in one of them his donkey should appear.

Now, though Apuleius loved eating and drinking, he was not at all fond of doing tricks in public, and as the day drew near he grew more and more resolved that he would take no part in the entertainment. So one warm moonlight night he stole out of his stable, and galloped as fast as he could for ten miles, when he reached the sea. He was hot and tired with his long run, and the sea looked cool and pleasant.

"It is years since I have had a bath," thought he, "or wetted anything but my feet. I will take one now; it will make me feel like a man again"; and into the water he went, and splashed about with joy, which would much have surprised any one who had seen him, for asses do not in general care about washing.

When he came back to dry land once more, he shook himself all over, and held his head first on one side and then on the other, so that the water might run out of his long ears. After that he felt quite comfortable, and lay down to sleep under a tree.

He was awakened some hours later by the sound of voices singing a hymn, and, raising his head, he saw a vast crowd of people trooping down to the shore to hold the festival of their goddess, and in their midst walked the high priest crowned with a wreath of roses.

At this sight hope was born afresh in the heart of Apuleius. It was long indeed since he had beheld any roses, for Thyasus fancied they made him ill, and would not suffer any one to grow them in the city. So he drew near to the priest as he passed by, and gazed at him so wistfully that, moved by some sudden impulse, the pontiff lifted the wreath from his head, and held it out to him, while the people drew to one side, feeling that something was happening which they did not understand.

Scarcely had Apuleius swallowed one of the roses, when the ass's skin fell from him, his back straightened itself, and his face once more became fair and rosy. Then he turned and joined in the hymn, and there was not a man among them all with a sweeter voice or more thankful spirit than that of Apuleius.

HOW ALEXANDER THE KING GOT THE WATER OF LIFE

THIS story is part of a longer one called "Alexander the Son of Philip." Alexander, a little bootblack living in modern Athens, is befriended by a blind old schoolmaster, Kyr Themistocli, to whom he promises to come each day and read the daily newspaper. For this service the little "Aleko" is to be helped with his lessons. By way of getting acquainted the old man asks, "Tell me, now, what do they call you?"

"They call me Aleko."

"From where?"

"My mother lives in Megaloupolis, and I was born there and the little ones, but my father was not from there."

Kyr Themistocli noticed the past tense.

"He is dead, your father?"

"Yes, it is two years ago that he died."

"And from where was he?"

"From Siatista."

"Ah, a Macedonian! And what was his name?"

"Philippos Vasiliou."

"So your name is Alexandros Vasiliou?"

Aleko nodded.

"Alexander of the King! Alexander the son of Philip! Your master has taught you about him at school?"

"Of course," said Aleko, frowning.

The old man smiled. There is a story about him which you have not heard perhaps. Do you know how Alexander the King got the Water of Life?"

Aleko shook his head: "We have not reached such a part."

"Well, I will tell you about it. Listen: —

"WHEN Alexander the King had conquered all the Kingdoms of the world, and when all the universe trembled at his glance, he called before him the most celebrated magicians of those days and said to them:

"'Ye who are wise, and who know all that is written in the Book of Fate, tell me what I must do to live for many years and to enjoy this world which I have made mine?'

"'O King!' said the magicians, 'great is thy power! But what is written in the Book of Fate is written, and no one in Heaven or on Earth can efface it. There is one thing only, that can make thee enjoy thy kingdom and thy glory beyond the lives of men; that can make thee endure as long as the hills, but it is very hard to accomplish.'

"'I did not ask ye,' said the great King Alexander, 'whether it be hard, I asked only what it was.'

"'O King, we are at thy feet to command! Know then that he alone who drinks of the Water of Life need not fear death. But he who seeks this water, must pass through two mountains which open and close constantly, and scarce a bird on the wing can fly between them and not be crushed to death. The bones lie in high piles, of the king's sons who have lost their lives in this terrible trap. But if thou shouldst pass safely through the closing mountains, even then thou wilt find beyond them a sleepless dragon who guards the Water of Life. Him also must thou slay before thou canst take the priceless treasure.'

"Then Alexander the King smiled, and ordered his slaves to bring forth his horse Bucephalus, who had no wings yet flew like a bird. The king mounted on his back and the good horse neighed for joy. With one triumphant bound he was through the closing mountains so swiftly that only three hairs of his flowing tail were caught in between the giant rocks when they closed. Then Alexander the King slew the sleepless dragon, filled his vial with the Water of Life, and returned.

"But when he reached his palace, so weary was he that he fell into a deep sleep and left the Water of Life unguarded. And it so happened that his sister, not knowing the value of the water, threw it away. And some of the water fell on a wild onion plant, and that is why, to this day, wild onion plants never fade. Now when Alexander awoke, he stretched out his hand to seize and drink the Water of Life and found naught; and in his rage he would have killed the slaves who guarded his sleep, but his sister being of royal blood, could not hide the truth, and she told him that, not knowing she had thrown the Water of Life away.

"Then the king waxed terrible in his wrath, and he cast a curse upon his sister, and prayed that from the waist downward she might be turned into a fish, and live always in the open sea far from all land and habitation of man. And the gods granted his prayer, so it happens that to this day those who sail over the open sea in ships often see Alexander's sister, half a woman and half a fish, tossing in the waves. Strange to say, she does not hate Alexander, and when a ship passes close to her she cries out: 'Does Alexander live?'

"And should the captain, not knowing who it is that speaks, answer, 'He is dead,' then the maid in her great grief tosses her white arms and her long golden hair wildly about, and troubles the water, and sinks the ship. But if, when the question comes up with the voice of the wind, 'Does Alexander live?' the captain answers at once, 'He lives and reigns,' then the maid's heart is joyful and she sings sweet songs till the ship is out of sight.

"And this is how sailors learn new love songs, and sing them when they return to land."

When the old man ceased speaking Aleko waited a moment and then said slowly:

"That is not true—but I like it."

AMERICAN INDIAN LEGENDS
THE FIRST CORN

A LONG time ago there lived in a Pawnee village a young man who was a great gambler. Every day he played at sticks, and he was almost always unlucky. Sometimes he would lose everything that he had, and would even lose things belonging to his father. His father had often scolded him about gambling, and had told him that he ought to stop it. There were two things that he never staked; these two things were his shield and his lance.

One day he played sticks for a long time, and when he got through he had lost everything that he had except these two things. When he went home at night to his father's lodge he told his relations what he had done, and his father said to him:

"My son, for a long time you have been doing this, and I have many times spoken to you about it. Now I have done. I cannot have you here any longer. You cannot live here in my lodge or in this village. You must go away."

The young man thought about it for a little while and then he said:

"Well, I will go. It does not make much difference where I am." So he took his shield and his spear and went out of the lodge and started to go away from the village. When he got outside of the village and had gone some distance, he heard behind him a loud rushing sound like a strong wind — the sound kept getting nearer and louder — and all at once it was above him, and then the sound stopped, and something spoke to him and said:

"Well, I am here. I have come to find you. I have been sent, and am here on purpose to get you and take you with me." The voice that spoke to him was the Wind.

The Wind took the young man up and carried him away towards the west. They traveled many days, and passed over broad prairies and then across high mountains and then over high, wide plains and over other mountains until they came to the end of the world, where the sky bends down and touches the ground. The last thing the young man saw was the gate through the edge of the sky. A great buffalo bull stands in this gateway and

110

blocks it up. He had to move to one side to let the Wind and the young man pass through. Every year one hair drops from the hide of this bull. When all have fallen the end of the world will come.

After they had passed through this gate they went on, and it seemed as if they were passing over a big water. There was nothing to be seen except the sky and the water. At last they came to a land. Here were many people—great crowds of them. The Wind told the young man:

"These are all waiters on the Father."

They went on, and at last came to the Father's lodge and went in. When they had sat down the Father spoke to the young man and said to him:

"My son, I have known you for a long time, and have watched you. I wanted to see you, and that is why I gave you bad luck at the sticks, and why I sent my Wind to bring you here. Your people are very hungry now because they can find no buffalo, but I am going to give you something on which you can live, even when the buffalo fail."

Then he gave him three little sacks. The first contained squash seed; the second beans, red and white; and the third corn, white, red, blue and yellow. The Father said:

"Tie these sacks to your shield and do not lose them. When you get back to your people give each one some of the seeds and tell him to put them in the ground; then they will make more. These things are good to eat, but the first year do not let the people eat them; let them put the yield away and the next year again put it in the ground. After that they can eat a part of what grows, but they must always save some for seed. So the people will always have something to eat with their buffalo meat, and something to depend on if the buffalo fail." The Father gave him also a buffalo robe, and said to him:

"When you go back, the next day after you have got there, call all the people together in your lodge, and give them what is in this robe, and tell them all these things. Now you can go back to your people."

The Wind took the young man back. They traveled a long time, and at last they came to the Pawnee village. The Wind put the young man down, and he went into his father's lodge and said:

"Father, I am here." But his father did not believe him, and said:

"It is not you." He had been gone so long that they had thought him dead. Then he said to his mother:

"Mother, I am here." And his mother knew him and was glad that he had returned.

At this time the people had no buffalo. They had scouted far and near and could find none anywhere, and they were all very hungry. The little children cried with hunger. The next day after he got back, the young man sent out an old man to go through the camp and call all the people to come to his father's lodge. When they were there, he opened his robe and spread it out, and it was covered with pieces of fat buffalo meat piled high. The young man gave to each person all he could carry, but while he was handing out the pieces, his father was trying to pull off the robe the hind-quarters of the buffalo and hide them. He was afraid that the young man might give away all the meat, and he wanted to save this for their own lodge. But the young man said:

"Father, do not take this away. Do not touch anything. There is enough."

After he had given them the meat he showed them the sacks of seed and told them what they were for, and explained to them that they must not eat any the first year, but that they must always save some to plant, and the people listened. Then he said to them:

"I hear that you have no buffalo. Come out to-morrow and I will show you where to go for buffalo." The People wondered where this could be, for they had traveled far in all directions looking for buffalo. The next day they went out as he had told them, and the young man sent two boys to the top of a high hill close to camp, and told them to let him know what they saw from it. When the boys got to the top of the hill, they saw down below them in the hollow a big band of buffalo.

When the people learned that the buffalo were there, they all took their arrows and ran out and chased the buffalo and made a big killing, so that there was plenty in the camp and they made much dried meat. Four days after this he again sent out the boys, and they found buffalo. Now that they had plenty of meat they stayed in one place, and when spring came the young man put the seed in the ground. When the people first saw these strange plants growing they wondered at them, for they were new and different from anything that they had ever seen growing on the prairie. They liked the color of the young stalks, and the way they tasseled out, and the way the ears formed. They found that besides being pretty to look at they were good to eat, for when the young man had gathered the crop he gave the people a little to taste, so that they might know the words that he had spoken were true. The rest he kept for seed. Next season he gave all the people seed to plant, and after that they always had these things.

Later, this young man became one of the head men, and taught the people many things. He told them that always when they killed buffalo they must bring the fattest and offer them to the Father. He taught them about the sacred bundles, and told them that they must put an ear of corn on the bundles and must keep a piece of fat in the bundles along with the corn, and that both must be kept out of sight. In the fall they should take the ear of corn out of the bundles and rub the piece of fat over it. Thus they would have good crops and plenty of food.

All these things the people did, and it was a help to them in their living.

WAUKEWA'S EAGLE

ONE day, when the Indian boy Waukewa was hunting along the mountain-side, he found a young eagle with a broken wing, lying at the base of a cliff. The bird had fallen from an aery on a ledge high above, and being too young to fly, had fluttered down the cliff and injured itself so severely that it was likely to die. When Waukewa saw it he was about to drive one of his sharp arrows through its body, for the passion of the hunter was strong in him, and the eagle plunders many a fine fish from the Indian's drying-frame. But a gentler impulse came to him as he saw the young bird quivering with pain and fright at his feet, and he slowly unbent his bow, put the arrow in his quiver, and stooped over the panting eaglet. For fully a minute the wild eyes of the wounded bird and the eyes of the Indian boy, growing gentler and softer as he gazed, looked into one another. Then the struggling and panting of the young eagle ceased; the wild, frightened look passed out of its eyes, and it suffered Waukewa to pass his hand gently over its ruffled and draggled feathers. The fierce instinct to fight, to defend its threatened life, yielded to the charm of the tenderness and pity expressed in the boy's eyes; and from that moment Waukewa and the eagle were friends.

Waukewa went slowly home to his father's lodge, bearing the wounded eaglet in his arms. He carried it so gently that the broken wing gave no twinge of pain, and the bird lay perfectly still, never offering to strike with its sharp beak the hands that clasped it.

Warming some water over the fire at the lodge, Waukewa bathed the broken wing of the eagle, and bound it up with soft strips of skin. Then he made a nest of ferns and grass inside the lodge, and laid the bird in it. The boy's mother looked on with shining eyes. Her heart was very tender. From girlhood she had loved all the creatures of the woods, and it pleased her to see some of her own gentle spirit waking in the boy.

When Waukewa's father returned from hunting, he would have caught up the young eagle and wrung its neck. But the boy pleaded with him so eagerly, stooping over the captive and defending it with his small hands, that the stern warrior laughed and called him his "little squaw-heart."

"Keep it, then," he said, "and nurse it until it is well. But then you must let it go, for we will not raise up a thief in the lodges." So Waukewa promised that when the eagle's wing was healed and grown so that it could fly, he would carry it forth and give it its freedom.

It was a month — or, as the Indians say, a moon — before the young eagle's wing had fully mended and the bird was old enough and strong enough to fly. And in the meantime Waukewa cared for it and fed it daily, and the friendship between the boy and the bird grew very strong.

But at last the time came when the willing captive must be freed. So Waukewa carried it far away from the Indian lodges, where none of the young braves might see it hovering over and be tempted to shoot their arrows at it, and there he let it go. The young eagle rose toward the sky in great circles, rejoicing in its freedom and its strange, new power of flight. But when Waukewa began to move away from the spot, it came swooping down again; and all day long it followed him through the woods as he hunted. At dusk, when Waukewa shaped his course for the Indian lodges, the eagle would have accompanied him. But the boy suddenly slipped into a hollow tree and hid, and after a long time the eagle stopped sweeping about in search of him and flew slowly and sadly away.

Summer passed, and then winter; and spring came again, with its flowers and birds and swarming fish in the lakes and streams. Then it was that all the Indians, old and young, braves and squaws, pushed their light canoes out from shore and with spear and hook waged pleasant war against the salmon and the red-spotted trout. After winter's long imprisonment, it was such joy to toss in the sunshine and the warm wind and catch savory fish to take the place of dried meats and corn!

Above the great falls of the Apahoqui the salmon sported in the cool, swinging current, darting under the lee of the rocks and leaping full length in the clear spring air. Nowhere else were such salmon to be speared as those which lay among the riffles at the head of the Apahoqui rapids. But only the most daring braves ventured to seek them there, for the current was strong, and should a light canoe once pass the danger-point and get

115

caught in the rush of the rapids, nothing could save it from going over the roaring falls.

Very early in the morning of a clear April day, just as the sun was rising splendidly over the mountains, Waukewa launched his canoe a half-mile above the rapids of the Apahoqui, and floated downward, spear in hand, among the salmon-riffles. He was the only one of the Indian lads who dared fish above the falls. But he had been there often, and never yet had his watchful eye and his strong paddle suffered the current to carry his canoe beyond the danger-point. This morning he was alone on the river, having risen long before daylight to be first at the sport.

The riffles were full of salmon, big, lusty fellows, who glided about the canoe on every side in an endless silver stream. Waukewa plunged his spear right and left, and tossed one glittering victim after another into the bark canoe. So absorbed in the sport was he that for once he did not notice when the canoe began to glide more swiftly among the rocks. But suddenly he looked up, caught his paddle, and dipped it wildly in the swirling water. The canoe swung sidewise, shivered, held its own against the torrent, and then slowly, inch by inch, began to creep upstream toward the shore. But suddenly there was a loud, cruel snap, and the paddle parted in the boy's hands, broken just above the blade! Waukewa gave a cry of despairing agony. Then he bent to the gunwale of his canoe and with the shattered blade fought desperately against the current. But it was useless. The racing torrent swept him downward; the hungry falls roared tauntingly in his ears.

Then the Indian boy knelt calmly upright in the canoe, facing the mist of the falls, and folded his arms. His young face was stern and lofty. He had lived like a brave hitherto—now he would die like one.

Faster and faster sped the doomed canoe toward the great cataract. The black rocks glided away on either side like phantoms. The roar of the terrible waters became like thunder in the boy's ears. But still he gazed calmly and sternly ahead, facing his fate as a brave Indian should. At last he began to chant the death-song, which he had learned from the older braves. In a few moments all would be over. But he would come before the Great Spirit with a fearless hymn upon his lips.

Suddenly a shadow fell across the canoe. Waukewa lifted his eyes and saw a great eagle hovering over, with dangling legs, and a spread of wings that blotted out the sun. Once more the eyes of the Indian boy and the eagle met; and now it was the eagle who was master!

With a glad cry the Indian boy stood up in his canoe, and the eagle hovered lower. Now the canoe tossed up on that great swelling wave that climbs to the cataract's edge, and the boy lifted his hands and caught the legs of the eagle. The next moment he looked down into the awful gulf of waters from its very verge. The canoe was snatched from beneath him and plunged down the black wall of the cataract; but he and the struggling eagle were floating outward and downwards through the cloud of mist. The cataract roared terribly, like a wild beast robbed of its prey. The spray beat and blinded, the air rushed upward as they fell. But the eagle struggled on with his burden. He fought his way out of the mist and the flying spray. His great wings threshed the air with a whistling sound. Down, down they sank, the boy and the eagle, but ever farther from the precipice of water and the boiling whirlpool below. At length, with a fluttering plunge, the eagle dropped on a sand-bar below the whirlpool, and he and the Indian boy lay there a minute, breathless and exhausted. Then the eagle slowly lifted himself, took the air under his free wings, and soared away, while the Indian boy knelt on the sand, with shining eyes following the great bird till he faded into the gray of the cliffs.

HALLOWE'EN AND MYSTERY STORIES
THE ROLL-CALL OF THE REEF

"YES, sir," said my host the quarryman, reaching down the relics from their hook in the wall over the chimney-piece; "they've hung there all my time, and most of my father's. The women won't touch 'em; they're afraid of the story. So here they'll dangle, and gather dust and smoke, till another tenant comes and tosses 'em out o' doors for rubbish. Whew! 'tis coarse weather."

He went to the door, opened it, and stood studying the gale that beat upon his cottage-front, straight from the Manacle Reef. The rain drove past him into the kitchen aslant like threads of gold silk in the shine of the wreckwood fire. Meanwhile by the same firelight I examined the relics on my knee. The metal of each was tarnished out of knowledge. But the trumpet was evidently an old cavalry trumpet, and the threads of its parti-colored sling, though frayed and dusty, still hung together. Around the side-drum, beneath its cracked brown varnish, I could hardly trace a royal coat-of-arms and a legend running, Per Mare per Terram — the motto of the Marines. Its parchment, though colored and scented with wood-smoke, was limp and mildewed, and I began to tighten up the straps — under which the drum-sticks had been loosely thrust — with the idle purpose of trying if some music might be got out of the old drum yet.

But as I turned it on my knee, I found the drum attached to the trumpet-sling by a curious barrel-shaped padlock, and paused to examine this. The body of the lock was composed of half a dozen brass rings, set accurately edge to edge; and, rubbing the brass with my thumb, I saw that each of the six had a series of letters engraved around it.

I knew the trick of it, I thought. Here was one of those word padlocks, once so common; only to be opened by getting the rings to spell a certain word, which the dealer confides to you.

My host shut and barred the door, and came back to the hearth.

"'Twas just such a wind — east by south — that brought in what you've got between your hands. Back in the year 'nine it was; my father has told me the tale a score o' times. You're twisting round the rings, I see. But you'll never guess the word. Parson Kendall, he made the word, and knocked down a couple o' ghosts in their graves with it, and when his time came, he went to his own grave and took the word with him."

"Whose ghosts, Matthew?"

"You want the story, I see, sir. My father could tell it better than I can. He was a young man in the year 'nine, unmarried at the time, and living in this very cottage just as I be. That's how he came to get mixed up with the tale."

He took a chair, lit a short pipe, and unfolded the story in a low musing voice, with his eyes fixed on the dancing violet flames.

"Yes, he'd ha' been about thirty year old in January of the year 'nine. The storm got up in the night o' the twenty-first o' that month. My father was dressed and out long before daylight; he never was one to 'bide in bed, let be that the gale by this time was pretty near lifting the thatch over his head. Besides which, he'd fenced a small 'taty-patch that winter, down by Lowland Point, and he wanted to see if it stood the night's work. He took the path across Gunner's Meadow — where they buried most of the bodies afterward. The wind was right in his teeth at the time, and once on the way (he's told me this often) a great strip of ore-weed came flying through the darkness and fetched him a slap on the cheek like a cold hand. But he made shift pretty well till he got to Lowland, and then had to drop upon his hands and knees and crawl, digging his fingers every now and then into the shingle to hold on, for he declared to me that the stones, some of them as big as a man's head, kept rolling and driving past till it seemed the whole foreshore was moving westward under him. The fence was gone, of course; not a stick left to show where it stood; so that, when first he came to the place, he thought he must have missed his bearings. My father, sir, was a very religious man; and if he reckoned the end of the world was at hand — there in the great wind and night, among the moving stones — you may believe he was certain of it when he heard a gun fired, and, with the same, saw a flame shoot up out of the darkness to windward, making a sudden fierce light in all the place about. All he could find to think or say was, 'The Second Coming — The Second Coming! The Bridegroom cometh, and the wicked He will toss like a ball into a large country!' and being already upon his knees, he just bowed his head and 'bided, saying this over and over.

"But by'm-by, between two squalls, he made bold to lift his head and look, and then by the light — a bluish color 'twas — he saw all the coast clear away to Manacle Point, and off the Manacles, in the thick of the weather, a sloop-of-war with top-gallants housed, driving stern foremost toward the reef. It was she, of course, that was burning the flare. My father could see the white streak and the ports of her quite plain as she rose to it, a little outside the breakers, and he guessed easy enough that her captain had just managed to wear ship, and was trying to force her nose to the sea with the help of her small bower anchor and the scrap or two of canvas that hadn't yet been blown out of her. But while he looked, she fell off, giving her broadside to it foot by foot, and drifting back on the breakers around Carn du and the Varses. The rocks lie so thick thereabouts, that 'twas a toss up which she struck first; at any rate, my father couldn't tell at the time, for just then the flare died down and went out.

"Well, sir, he turned then in the dark and started back for Coverack to cry the dismal tidings — though well knowing ship and crew to be past any hope; and as he turned, the wind lifted him and tossed him forward 'like a ball,' as he'd been saying, and homeward along the foreshore. As you know, 'tis ugly work, even by daylight, picking your way among the stones there, and my father was prettily knocked about at first in the dark. But by this 'twas nearer seven than six o'clock, and the day spreading. By the time he reached North Corner, a man could see to read print; hows'ever he looked neither out to sea nor toward Coverack, but headed straight for the first cottage — the same that stands above North Corner to-day. A man named Billy Ede lived there then, and when my father burst into the kitchen bawling, 'Wreck! wreck!' he saw Billy Ede's wife, Ann, standing there in her clogs, with a shawl over her head, and her clothes wringing wet.

"'Save the chap!' says Billy Ede's wife, Ann. 'What d' 'ee means by crying stale fish at that rate?'

"'But 'tis a wreck. I tell 'ee. I've azeed'n!'

"'Why, so 'tis,' says she, 'and I've azeed'n, too; and so has every one with an eye in his head.'

"And with that she pointed straight over my father's shoulder, and he turned: and there, close under Dolor Point, at the end of Coverack town, he saw another wreck washing, and the Point black with people, like emmets, running to and fro in the morning light. While we stood staring at her, he heard a trumpet sounded on board, the notes coming in little jerks, like a bird rising against the wind; but faintly, of course, because of the distance and the gale blowing — though this had dropped a little.

"'She's a transport,' said Billy Ede's wife, Ann, 'and full of horse soldiers, fine long men. When she struck they must ha' pitched the hosses over first to lighten the ship, for a score of dead hosses had washed in afore I left, half an hour back. An' three or four soldiers, too — fine long corpses in white breeches and jackets of blue and gold. I held the lantern to one. Such a straight young man.'

"My father asked her about the trumpeting.

"'That's the queerest bit of all. She was burnin' a light when me an' my man joined the crowd down there. All her masts had gone; whether they were carried away, or were cut away to ease her, I don't rightly know. Anyway, there she lay 'pon the rocks with her decks bare. Her keelson was broke under her and her bottom sagged and stove, and she had just settled down like a sitting hen — just the leastest list to starboard; but a man could stand there easy. They had rigged up ropes across her, from bulwark to bulwark, an' beside these the men were mustered, holding on like grim death whenever the sea made a clean breach over them, an' standing up like heroes as soon as it passed. The captain an' the officers were clinging to the rail of the quarter-deck, all in their golden uniforms, waiting for the end as if 'twas King George they expected. There was no way to help, for she lay right beyond cast of line, though our folk tried it fifty times. And beside them clung a trumpeter, a whacking big man, an' between the heavy seas he would lift his trumpet with one hand, and blow a call; and every time he blew the men gave a cheer. There (she says) — hark 'ee now — there he goes agen! But you won't hear no cheering any more, for few are left to cheer, and their voices weak. Bitter cold the wind is, and I reckon it numbs their grip o' the ropes, for they were dropping off fast with every sea when my man sent me home to get his breakfast. Another wreck, you say? Well, there's no hope for the tender dears, if 'tis the Manacles. You'd better run down and help yonder; though 'tis little help that any man can give. Not one came in alive while I was there. The tide's flowing, an' she won't hold together another hour, they say.'

"Well, sure enough, the end was coming fast when my father got down to the point. Six men had been cast up alive, or just breathing — a seaman and five troopers. The seaman was the only one that had breath to speak; and while they were carrying him into the town, the word went round that the ship's name was the Despatch, transport, homeward bound from Corunna, with a detachment of the 7th Hussars, that had been fighting out there with Sir John Moore. The seas had rolled her farther over by this time, and given her decks a pretty sharp slope; but a dozen men still held on, seven by the ropes near the ship's waist, a couple near the break of the poop, and three on the quarter-deck. Of these three my father made out one to be the skipper; close by him clung an officer in full regimentals — his name, they heard after, was Captain Duncanfield; and last came the tall trumpeter; and if you'll believe me, the fellow was making shift there, at the very last, to blow 'God Save the King.' What's more, he got to 'Send Us Victorious' before an extra big sea came bursting across and washed them off the deck — every man but one of the pair beneath the poop — and he dropped his hold before the next wave; being stunned, I reckon. The others went out of sight at once, but the trumpeter — being, as I said, a powerful man as well as a tough swimmer — rose like a duck, rode out a couple of breakers, and came in on the crest of the third. The folks looked to see him broke like an egg at their feet; but when the smother cleared, there he was, lying face downward on a ledge below them; and one of the men that happened to have a rope round him — I forget the fellow's name, if I ever heard it — jumped down and grabbed him by the ankle as he began to slip back. Before the next big sea, the pair were hauled high enough to be out of harm, and another heave brought them up to grass. Quick work; but master trumpeter wasn't quite dead! nothing worse than a cracked head and three staved ribs. In twenty minutes or so they had him in bed, with the doctor to tend him.

"Now was the time—nothing being left alive upon the transport—for my father to tell of the sloop he'd seen driving upon the Manacles. And when he got a hearing, though the most were set upon salvage, and believed a wreck in the hand, so to say, to be worth half a dozen they couldn't see, a good few volunteered to start off with him and have a look. They crossed Lowland Point; no ship to be seen on the Manacles, nor anywhere upon the sea. One or two was for calling my father a liar. 'Wait till we come to Dean Point,' said he. Sure enough, on the far side of Dean Point, they found the sloop's mainmast washing about with half a dozen men lashed to it—men in red jackets—every mother's son drowned and staring; and a little farther on, just under the Dean, three or four bodies cast up on the shore, one of them a small drummer-boy, side-drum and all; and, near by, part of a ship's gig, with 'H. M. S. Primrose' cut on the stern-board. From this point on, the shore was littered thick with wreckage and dead bodies—the most of them marines in uniform; and in Godrevy Cove in particular, a heap of furniture from the captain's cabin, and among it a water-tight box, not much damaged, and full of papers, by which, when it came to be examined next day, the wreck was easily made out to be the Primrose of eighteen guns, outward bound from Portsmouth, with a fleet of transports for the Spanish War, thirty sail, I've heard, but I've never heard what became of them. Being handled by merchant skippers, no doubt they rode out the gale and reached the Tagus safe and sound. Not but what the captain of the Primrose (Mein was his name) did quite right to try and club-haul his vessel when he found himself under the land; only he never ought to have got there if he took proper soundings. But it's easy talking.

"The Primrose, sir, was a handsome vessel—for her size, one of the handsomest in the King's service—and newly fitted out at Plymouth Dock. So the boys had brave pickings from her in the way of brass-work, ship's instruments, and the like, let alone some barrels of stores not much spoiled. They loaded themselves with as much as they could carry, and started for home, meaning to make a second journey before the preventive men got wind of their doings and came to spoil the fun. But as my father was passing back under the Dean, he happened to take a look over his shoulder at the bodies there. 'Hullo,' says he, and dropped his gear, 'I do believe there's a leg moving!' And, running fore, he stooped over the small drummer-boy that I told you about. The poor little chap was lying there, with his face a mass of bruises and his eyes closed: but he had shifted one leg an inch or two, and was still breathing. So my father pulled out a knife and cut him free from his drum — that was lashed on to him with a double turn of Manilla rope — and took him up and carried him along here, to this very room that we're sitting in. He lost a good deal by this, for when he went back to fetch his bundle the preventive men had got hold of it, and were thick as thieves along the foreshore; so that 'twas only by paying one or two to look the other way that he picked up anything worth carrying off: which you'll allow to be hard, seeing that he was the first man to give news of the wreck.

"Well, the inquiry was held, of course, and my father gave evidence, and for the rest they had to trust to the sloop's papers, for not a soul was saved besides the drummer-boy, and he was raving in a fever, brought on by the cold and the fright. And the seamen and the five troopers gave evidence about the loss of the Despatch. The tall trumpeter, too, whose ribs were healing, came forward and kissed the book; but somehow his head had been hurt in coming ashore, and he talked foolish-like, and 'twas easy seen he would never be a proper man again. The others were taken up to Plymouth, and so went their ways; but the trumpeter stayed on in Coverick; and King George, finding he was fit for nothing, sent him down a trifle of a pension after a while — enough to keep him in board and lodging, with a bit of tobacco over.

"Now the first time that this man — William Tallifer, he called himself — met with the drummer-boy, was about a fortnight after the little chap had bettered enough to be allowed a short walk out of doors, which he took, if you please, in full regimentals. There never was a soldier so proud of his dress. His own suit had shrunk a brave bit with the salt water; but into ordinary frock an' corduroys he declared he would not get — not if he had to go naked the rest of his life; so my father, being a good-natured man and handy with the needle, turned to and repaired damages with a piece or two of scarlet cloth cut from the jacket of one of the drowned Marines. Well, the poor little chap chanced to be standing, in this rig-out, down by the gate of Gunner's Meadow, where they had buried two-score and over of his comrades. The morning was a fine one, early in March month; and along came the cracked trumpeter, likewise taking a stroll.

"'Hullo!' says he; 'good-mornin'! And what might you be doin' here?'

"'I was a-wishin',' says the boy, 'I had a pair o' drumsticks. Our lads were buried yonder without so much as a drum tapped or a musket fired; and that's not Christian burial for British soldiers.'

"'Phut!' says the trumpeter, and spat on the ground; 'a parcel of Marines!'

"The boy eyed him a second or so, but answered up: 'If I'd a tab of turf handy, I'd bung it at your mouth, you greasy cavalryman, and learn you to speak respectful of your betters. The Marines are the handiest body of men in the service.'

"The trumpeter looked down on him from the height of six foot two, and asked: 'Did they die well?'

"'They died very well. There was a lot of running to and fro at first, and some of the men began to cry, and a few to strip off their clothes. But when the ship fell off for the last time, Captain Mein turned and said something to Major Griffiths, the commanding officer on board, and the Major called out to me to beat to quarters. It might have been for a wedding, he sang it out so cheerful. We'd had word already that 'twas to be parade order, and the men fell in as trim and decent as if they were going to church. One or two even tried to shave at the last moment. The Major wore his medals. One of the seamen, seeing that I had hard work to keep the drum steady — the sling being a bit loose for me and the wind what you remember — lashed it tight with a piece of rope; and that saved my life afterward, a drum being as good as a cork until it's stove. I kept beating away until every man was on deck; and then the Major formed them up and told them to die like British soldiers, and the chaplain read a prayer or two — the boys standin' all the while like rocks, each man's courage keeping up the other's. The chaplain was in the middle of a prayer when she struck. In ten minutes she was gone. That was how they died, cavalryman.'

"'And that was very well done, drummer of the Marines. What's your name?'

"'John Christian.'

"'Mine's William George Tallifer, trumpeter, of the 7th Light Dragoons — the Queen's Own. I played 'God Save the King' while our men were drowning. Captain Duncanfield told me to sound a call or two, to put them in heart; but that matter of 'God Save the King' was a notion of my own. I won't say anything to hurt the feelings of a Marine, even if he's not much over five foot tall; but the Queen's Own Hussars is a tearin' fine regiment. As between horse and foot 'tis a question o' which gets the chance. All the way from Sahagun to Corunna 'twas we that took and gave the knocks — at Mayorga and Rueda and Bennyventy.' (The reason, sir, I can speak the names so pat is that my father learnt 'em by heart afterward from the trumpeter, who was always talking about Mayorga and Rueda and Bennyventy.) 'We made the rearguard, under General Paget, and drove the French every time; and all the infantry did was to sit about in wine-shops till we whipped 'em out, an' steal an' straggle an' play the tom-fool in general. And when it came to a stand-up fight at Corunna, 'twas we that had to stay sea-sick aboard the transports, an' watch the infantry in the thick o' the caper. Very well they behaved, too; 'specially the 4th Regiment, an' the 42d Highlanders, an' the Dirty Half-Hundred. Oh, ay; they're decent regiments, all three. But the Queen's Own Hussars is a tearin' fine regiment. So you played on your drum when the ship was goin' down? Drummer John Christian, I'll have to get you a new pair o' drum-sticks for that.'

"Well, sir, it appears that the very next day the trumpeter marched into Helston, and got a carpenter there to turn him a pair of box-wood drum-sticks for the boy. And this was the beginning of one of the most curious friendships you ever heard tell of. Nothing delighted the pair more than to borrow a boat of my father and pull out to the rocks where the Primrose and the Despatch had struck and sunk; and on still days 'twas pretty to hear them out there off the Manacles, the drummer playing his tattoo — for they always took their music with them — and the trumpeter practising calls, and making his trumpet speak like an angel. But if the weather turned roughish, they'd be walking together and talking; leastwise, the youngster listened while the other discoursed about Sir John's campaign in Spain and Portugal, telling how each little skirmish befell; and of Sir John himself, and General Baird and General Paget, and Colonel Vivian his own commanding officer, and what kind men they were; and of the last bloody stand-up at Corunna, and so forth, as if neither could have enough.

"But all this had to come to an end in the late summer, for the boy, John Christian, being now well and strong again, must go up to Plymouth to report himself. 'Twas his own wish (for I believe King George had forgotten all about him), but his friend wouldn't hold him back. As for the trumpeter, my father had made an arrangement to take him on as a lodger as soon as the boy left; and on the morning fixed for the start he was up at the door here by five o'clock, with his trumpet slung by his side, and all the rest of his belongings in a small valise. A Monday morning it was, and after breakfast he had fixed to walk with the boy some way on the road toward Helston, where the coach started. My father left them at breakfast together, and went out to meat the pig, and do a few odd morning jobs of that sort. When he came back, the boy was still at table, and the trumpeter standing here by the chimney-place with the drum and trumpet in his hands, hitched together just as they be at this moment.

"'Look at this,' he says to my father, showing him the lock; 'I picked it up off a starving brass-worker in Lisbon, and it is not one of your common locks that one word of six letters will open at any time. There's janius in this lock; for you've only to make the ring spell any six-letter word you please, and snap down the lock upon that, and never a soul can open it — not the maker, even — until somebody comes along that knows the word you snapped it on. Now, Johnny, here's goin', and he leaves his drum behind him; for, though he can make pretty music on it, the parchment sags in wet weather, by reason of the sea-water getting at it; an' if he carries it to Plymouth, they'll only condemn it and give him another. And as for me, I shan't have the heart to put lip to the trumpet any more when Johnny's gone. So we've chosen a word together, and locked 'em together upon that; and, by your leave, I'll hang 'em here together on the hook over your fireplace. Maybe Johnny'll come back; maybe not. Maybe, if he comes, I'll be dead an' gone, an' he'll take 'em apart an' try their music for old sake's sake. But if he never comes, nobody can separate 'em; for nobody besides knows the word. And if you marry and have sons, you can tell 'em that here are tied together the souls of Johnny Christian, drummer, of the Marines, and William George Tallifer, once trumpeter of the Queen's Own Hussars. Amen.'

"With that he hung the two instruments 'pon the hook there; and the boy stood up and thanked my father and shook hands; and the pair went forth of the door, toward Helston.

"Somewhere on the road they took leave of one another; but nobody saw the parting, nor heard what was said between them. About three in the afternoon the trumpeter came walking back over the hill; and by the time my father came home from the fishing, the cottage was tidied up and the tea ready, and the whole place shining like a new pin. From that time for five years he lodged here with my father, looking after the house and tilling the garden; and all the while he was steadily failing, the hurt in his head spreading, in a manner, to his limbs. My father watched the feebleness growing on him, but said nothing. And from first to last neither spake a word about the drummer, John Christian; nor did any letter reach them, nor word of his doings.

"The rest of the tale you'm free to believe, sir, or not, as you please. It stands upon my father's words, and he always declared he was ready to kiss the Book upon it before judge and jury. He said, too, that he never had the wit to make up such a yarn; and he defied any one to explain about the lock, in particular, by any other tale. But you shall judge for yourself.

"My father said that about three o'clock in the morning, April fourteenth of the year 'fourteen, he and William Tallifer were sitting here, just as you and I, sir, are sitting now. My father had put on his clothes a few minutes before, and was mending his spiller by the light of the horn lantern, meaning to set off before daylight to haul the trammel. The trumpeter hadn't been to bed at all. Toward the last he mostly spent his nights (and his days, too) dozing in the elbow-chair where you sit at this minute. He was dozing then (my father said), with his chin dropped forward on his chest, when a knock sounded upon the door, and the door opened, and in walked an upright young man in scarlet regimentals.

"He had grown a brave bit, and his face was the color of wood-ashes; but it was the drummer, John Christian. Only his uniform was different from the one he used to wear, and the figures '38' shone in brass upon his collar.

"The drummer walked past my father as if he never saw him, and stood by the elbow-chair and said:

"'Trumpeter, trumpeter, are you one with me?'

"And the trumpeter just lifted the lids of his eyes, and answered, 'How should I not be one with you, drummer Johnny—Johnny boy? The men are patient. 'Til you come, I count; you march, I mark time until the discharge comes.'

"'The discharge has come to-night,' said the drummer, 'and the word is Corunna no longer;' and stepping to the chimney-place, he unhooked the drum and trumpet, and began to twist the brass rings of the lock, spelling the word aloud, so—C-O-R-U-N-A. When he had fixed the last letter, the padlock opened in his hand.

"'Did you know, trumpeter, that when I came to Plymouth they put me into a line regiment.'

"'The 38th is a good regiment,' answered the old Hussar, still in his dull voice. 'I went back with them from Sahagun to Corunna. At Corunna they stood in General Fraser's division, on the right. They behaved well.'

"'But I'd fain see the Marines again,' says the drummer, handing him the trumpet, 'and you—you shall call once more for the Queen's Own. Matthew,' he says, suddenly, turning on my father—and when he turned, my father saw for the first time that his scarlet jacket had a round hole by the breast-bone, and that the blood was welling there—'Matthew, we shall want your boat.'

"Then my father rose on his legs like a man in a dream, while they two slung on, the one his drum, and t'other his trumpet. He took the lantern, and went quaking before them down to the shore, and they breathed heavily behind him; and they stepped into his boat, and my father pushed off.

"'Row you first for Dolor Point,' says the drummer. So my father rowed them out past the white houses of Coverack to Dolor Point, and there, at a word, lay on his oars. And the trumpeter, William Tallifer, put his trumpet to his mouth and sounded the Revelly. The music of it was like rivers running.

"'They will follow,' said the drummer. 'Matthew, pull you now for the Manacles.'

"So my father pulled for the Manacles, and came to an easy close outside Carn du. And the drummer took his sticks and beat a tattoo, there by the edge of the reef; and the music of it was like a rolling chariot.

"'That will do,' says he, breaking off; 'they will follow. Pull now for the shore under Gunner's Meadow.'

"Then my father pulled for the shore, and ran his boat in under Gunner's Meadow. And they stepped out, all three, and walked up to the meadow. By the gate the drummer halted and began his tattoo again, looking out toward the darkness over the sea.

"And while the drum beat, and my father held his breath, there came up out of the sea and the darkness a troop of many men, horse and foot, and formed up among the graves; and others rose out of the graves and formed up—drowned Marines with bleached faces, and pale Hussars riding their horses, all lean and shadowy. There was no clatter of hoofs or accoutrements, my father said, but a soft sound all the while, like the beating of a bird's wing and a black shadow lying like a pool about the feet of all. The drummer stood upon a little knoll just inside the gate, and beside him the tall trumpeter, with hand on hip, watching them gather;

and behind them both my father, clinging to the gate. When no more came the drummer stopped playing, and said, 'Call the roll.'

"Then the trumpeter stepped toward the end man of the rank and called, 'Troop-Sergeant-Major Thomas Irons,' and the man in a thin voice answered, 'Here!'

"'Troop-Sergeant-Major Thomas Irons, how is it with you?'

"The man answered, 'How should it be with me? When I was young, I betrayed a girl; and when I was grown, I betrayed a friend, and for these things I must pay. But I died as a man ought. God save the King!'

"The trumpeter called to the next man, 'Trooper Henry Buckingham', and the next man answered, 'Here!'

"'Trooper Henry Buckingham, how is it with you?'

"'How should it be with me? I was a drunkard, and I stole, and in Lugo, in a wine-shop, I knifed a man. But I died as a man should. God save the King!'

"So the trumpeter went down the line; and when he had finished, the drummer took it up, hailing the dead Marines in their order. Each man answered to his name, and each man ended with 'God save the King!' When all were hailed, the drummer stepped back to his mound, and called:

"'It is well. You are content, and we are content to join you. Wait yet a little while.'

"With this he turned and ordered my father to pick up the lantern, and lead the way back. As my father picked it up, he heard the ranks of dead men cheer and call, 'God save the King!' all together, and saw them waver and fade back into the dark, like a breath fading off a pane.

"But when they came back here to the kitchen, and my father set the lantern down, it seemed they'd both forgot about him. For the drummer turned in the lantern-light—and my father could see the blood still welling out of the hole in his breast—and took the trumpet-sling from around the other's neck, and locked drum and trumpet together again, choosing the letters on the lock very carefully. While he did this he said:

"'The word is no more Corunna, but Bayonne. As you left out an "n" in Corunna, so must I leave out an "n" in Bayonne.' And before snapping the padlock, he spelt out the word slowly — 'B-A-Y-O-N-E.' After that, he used no more speech; but turned and hung the two instruments back on the hook; and then took the trumpeter by the arm; and the pair walked out into the darkness, glancing neither to right nor left.

"My father was on the point of following, when he heard a sort of sigh behind him; and there, sitting in the elbow-chair, was the very trumpeter he had just seen walk out by the door! If my father's heart jumped before, you may believe it jumped quicker now. But after a bit, he went up to the man asleep in the chair, and put a hand upon him. It was the trumpeter in flesh and blood that he touched; but though the flesh was warm, the trumpeter was dead.

"Well, sir, they buried him three days after; and at first my father was minded to say nothing about his dream (as he thought it). But the day after the funeral, he met Parson Kendall coming from Helston market: and the parson called out: 'Have 'ee heard the news the coach brought down this mornin'?' 'What news?' says my father. 'Why, that peace is agreed upon.' 'None too soon,' says my father. 'Not soon enough for our poor lads at Bayonne,' the parson answered. 'Bayonne!' cries my father, with a jump. 'Why, yes;' and the parson told him all about a great sally the French had made on the night of April 13th. 'Do you happen to know if the 38th Regiment was engaged?' my father asked. 'Come, now,' said Parson Kendall, 'I didn't know you was so well up in the campaign. But, as it happens, I do know that the 38th was engaged, for 'twas they that held a cottage and stopped the French advance.'

"Still my father held his tongue; and when, a week later, he walked into Helston and bought a Mercury off the Sherborne rider, and got the landlord of the Angel to spell out the list of killed and wounded, sure enough, there among the killed was Drummer John Christian, of the 38th Foot.

"After this there was nothing for a religious man but to make a clean breast. So my father went up to Parson Kendall and told the whole story. The parson listened, and put a question or two, and then asked:

"'Have you tried to open the lock since that night?'

"'I han't dared to touch it,' says my father.

"'Then come along and try.' When the parson came to the cottage here, he took the things off the hook and tried the lock. 'Did he say "Bayonne"? The word has seven letters.'

"'Not if you spell it with one "n" as he did,' says my father.

"The parson spelt it out—B-A-Y-O-N-E. 'Whew!' says he, for the lock had fallen open in his hand.

"He stood considering it a moment, and then he said, 'I tell you what. I shouldn't blab this all round the parish, if I was you. You won't get no credit for truth-telling, and a miracle's wasted on a set of fools. But if you like, I'll shut down the lock again upon a holy word that no one but me shall know, and neither drummer nor trumpeter, dead nor alive, shall frighten the secret out of me.'

"'I wish to gracious you would, parson,' said my father.

"The parson chose the holy word there and then, and shut the lock back upon it, and hung the drum and trumpet back in their place. He is gone long since, taking the word with him. And till the lock is broken by force, nobody will ever separate those twain."

HOW JAN BREWER WAS PISKEY-LADEN

THE moon was near her setting as a tall, broad-shouldered man called Jan Brewer was walking home to Constantine Bay to his cottage on the edge of the cliff.

He was singing an old song to himself as he went along, and he sang till he drew near the ruins of Constantine Church, standing on a sandy common near the bay. As he drew near the remains of this ancient church, which were clearly seen in the moonshine, he thought he heard some one laughing, but he was not quite sure, for the sea was roaring on the beach below the common, and the waves were making a loud noise as they dashed up the great headland of Trevose.

"I was mistaken; 'twas nobody laughing," said Jan to himself, and he walked on again, singing as before; and he sang till he came near a gate, which opened into a field leading to his cottage, but when he got there he could not see the gate or the gateway.

"I was so taken up with singing the old song, that I must have missed my way," he said again to himself. "I'll go back to the head of the common and start afresh," which he did; and when he got to the place where his gate ought to have been, he could not find it to save his life.

"I must be clean mazed," he cried. "I have never got out of my reckoning before, nor missed finding my way to our gate, even when the night has been as dark as pitch. It isn't at all dark to-night; I can see Trevose Head — and yet I can't see my own little gate! But I en't a-going to be done; I'll go round and round this common till I do find my gate."

And round and round the common he went, but find his gate he could not.

Every time he passed the ruins of the church a laugh came up from the pool below the ruins, and once he thought he saw a dancing light on the edge of the pool, where a lot of reeds and rushes were growing.

"The Little Man in the Lantern is about to-night," he said to himself, as he glanced at the pool. "But I never knew he was given to laughing before."

Once more he went round the common, and when he had passed the ruins he heard giggling and laughing, this time quite close to him; and looking down on the grass, he saw to his astonishment hundreds of Little Men and Little Women with tiny lights in their hands, which they were flinking about as they laughed and giggled.

The Little Men wore stocking-caps, the color of ripe briar berries, and grass-green coats, and the Little Women had on old grandmother cloaks of the same vivid hue as the Wee Men's coats, and they also wore little scarlet hoods.

"I believe the great big chap sees us," said one of the Little Men, catching sight of Jan's astonished face. "He must be Piskey-eyed, and we did not know it."

"Is he really?" cried one of the Dinky Women. "'Tis a pity, but we'll have our game over him just the same."

"That we will," cried all the Little Men and Little Women in one voice; and, forming a ring round the great tall fellow, they began to dance round him, laughing, giggling and flashing up their lights as they danced.

They went round him so fast that poor Jan was quite bewildered, and whichever way he looked there were these Little Men and Little Women giggling up into his bearded face. And when he tried to break through their ring they went before him and behind him, making a game over him.

He was at their mercy and they knew it; and when they saw the great fellow's misery, they only laughed and giggled the more.

"We've got him!" they cried to each other, and they said it with such gusto and with such a comical expression on their tiny brown faces, that Jan, bewildered as he was, and tired with going round the common so many times, could not help laughing, they looked so very funny, particularly when the Little Women winked up at him from under their little scarlet hoods.

The Piskeys—for they were Piskeys—hurried him down the common, dancing round him all the time; and when he got there he felt so mizzy-mazey with those tiny whirling figures going round and round him like a whirligig, that he did not know whether he was standing on his head or his heels. He was also in a bath of perspiration — "sweating leaking," he said — and, putting his hand in his pocket to take out a handkerchief to mop his face, he remembered having been told that, if he ever got Piskey-laden, he must turn his coat pockets inside out, then he would be free at once from his Piskey tormentors. And in a minute or less his coat-pockets were hanging out, and all the Little Men and the Little Women had vanished, and there, right in front of him, he saw his own gate! He lost no time in opening it, and in a very short time was in his thatched cottage on the cliff.

MY GRANDFATHER, HENDRY WATTY

A DROLL

'TIS the nicest miss in the world that I was born grandson of my own father's father, and not of another man altogether.

Hendry Watty was the name of my grandfather that might have been; and he always maintained that to all intents and purposes he was my grandfather, and made me call him so — 'twas such a narrow shave. I don't mind telling you about it. 'Tis a curious tale, too.

My grandfather, Hendry Watty, bet four gallons of eggy-hot that he would row out to the Shivering Grounds, all in the dead waste of the night, and haul a trammel there. To find the Shivering Grounds by night, you get the Gull Rock in a line with Tregamenna and pull out till you open the light on St. Anthony's Point; but everybody gives the place a wide berth because Archelaus Rowett's lugger foundered there one time, with six hands on board; and they say that at night you can hear the drowned men hailing their names. But my grandfather was the boldest man in Port Loe, and said he didn't care. So one Christmas Eve by daylight he and his mates went out and tilled the trammel; and then they came back and spent the forepart of the evening over the eggy-hot, down to Oliver's tiddly-wink, to keep my grandfather's spirits up and also to show that the bet was made in earnest.

'Twas past eleven o'clock when they left Oliver's and walked down to the cove to see my grandfather off. He has told me since that he didn't feel afraid at all, but very friendly in mind, especially toward William John Dunn, who was walking on his right hand. This puzzled him at the first, for as a rule he didn't think much of William John Dunn. But now he shook hands with him several times, and just as he was stepping into the boat he says, "You'll take care of Mary Polly while I'm away." Mary Polly Polsue was my grandfather's sweetheart at that time. But why my grandfather should have spoken as if he was bound on a long voyage he never could tell; he used to set it down to fate.

"I will," said William John Dunn; and then they gave a cheer and pushed my grandfather off, and he lit his pipe and away he rowed all into the dead waste of the night. He rowed and rowed, all in the dead waste the night; and he got the Gull Rock in a line with Tregamenna windows; and still he was rowing, when to his great surprise he heard a voice calling:

"Hendry Watty! Hendry Watty!"

I told you my grandfather was the boldest man in Port Loe. But he dropped his two oars now, and made the five signs of Penitence. For who could it be calling him out here in the dead waste and middle of the night?

"HENDRY WATTY! HENDRY WATTY! drop

me a line."

My grandfather kept his fishing-lines in a little skivet under the stern-sheets. But not a trace of bait had he on board. If he had, he was too much a-tremble to bait a hook.

"HENDRY WATTY! HENDRY WATTY! drop

me a line, or I'll know why."

My poor grandfather had by this picked up his oars again, and was rowing like mad to get quit of the neighborhood, when something or somebody gave three knocks—thump, thump, thump!—on the bottom of the boat, just as you would knock on a door.

The third thump fetched Hendry Watty upright on his legs. He had no more heart for disobeying, but having bitten his pipe-stem in half by this time—his teeth chattered so—he baited his hook with the broken bit and flung it overboard, letting the line run out in the stern-notch. Not half-way had it run before he felt a long pull on it, like the sucking of a dog-fish.

"Hendry Watty! Hendry Watty! pull me in."

Hendry Watty pulled in hand over fist, and in came the lead sinker over the notch, and still the line was heavy; he pulled and he pulled, and next, all out of the dead waste of the night, came two white hands, like a washerwoman's, and gripped hold of the stern-board; and on the left of these two hands, was a silver ring, sunk very deep in the flesh. If this was bad, worse was the face that followed—and if this was bad for anybody, it was worse for my grandfather who had known Archelaus Rowett before he was drowned out on the Shivering Grounds, six years before.

Archelaus Rowett climbed in over the stern, pulled the hook with the bit of pipe-stem out of his cheek, sat down in the stern-sheets, shook a small crayfish out of his whiskers, and said very coolly: "If you should come across my wife —"

That was all that my grandfather stayed to hear. At the sound of Archelaus's voice he fetched a yell, jumped clean over the side of the boat and swam for dear life. He swam and swam, till by the bit of the moon he saw the Gull Rock close ahead. There were lashin's of rats on the Gull Rock, as he knew; but he was a good deal surprised at the way they were behaving, for they sat in a row at the water's edge and fished, with their tails let down into the sea for fishing-lines; and their eyes were like garnets burning as they looked at my grandfather over their shoulders.

"Hendry Watty! Hendry Watty! you can't land here — you're disturbing the pollack."

"Bejimbers! I wouldn' do that for the world," says my grandfather; so off he pushes and swims for the mainland. This was a long job, and it was as much as he could do to reach Kibberick beach, where he fell on his face and hands among the stones, and there lay, taking breath.

The breath was hardly back in his body before he heard footsteps, and along the beach came a woman, and passed close by to him. He lay very quiet, and as she came near he saw 'twas Sarah Rowett, that used to be Archelaus's wife, but had married another man since. She was knitting as she went by, and did not seem to notice my grandfather; but he heard her say to herself, "The hour is come, and the man is come."

He had scarcely begun to wonder over this when he spied a ball of worsted yarn beside him that Sarah had dropped. 'Twas the ball she was knitting from, and a line of worsted stretched after her along the beach. Hendry Watty picked up the ball and followed the thread on tiptoe. In less than a minute he came near enough to watch what she was doing; and what she did was worth watching. First she gathered wreckwood and straw, and struck flint over touchwood and teened a fire. Then she unraveled her knitting; twisted her end of the yarn between finger and thumb—like a cobbler twisting a wax-end—and cast the end up towards the sky. It made Hendry Watty stare when the thread, instead of falling back to the ground, remained hanging, just as if 'twas fastened to something up above; but it made him stare still more when Sarah Rowett began to climb up it, and away up till nothing could be seen of her but her ankles dangling out of the dead waste and middle of the night.

"Hendry Watty! Hendry Watty!"

It wasn't Sarah calling, but a voice far away out to sea.

"Hendry Watty! Hendry Watty! Send

me a line!"

My grandfather was wondering what to do, when Sarah speaks down very sharp to him, out of the dark:

"Hendry Watty! where's the rocket apparatus? Can't you hear the poor fellow asking for a line?"

"I do," says my grandfather, who was beginning to lose his temper; "and do you think, ma'am, that I carry a Boxer's rocket in my trousers pocket?"

"I think you have a ball of worsted in your hand," says she. "Throw it as far as you can."

So my grandfather threw the ball out into the dead waste and middle of the night. He didn't see where it pitched, or how far it went.

"Right it is," says the woman aloft. "'Tis easy seen you're a hurler. But what shall us do for a cradle? Hendry Watty! Hendry Watty!"

"Ma'am to you," said my grandfather.

"If you have the common feelings of a gentleman, I'll ask you to turn your back; I'm going to take off my stocking."

So my grandfather stared the other way very politely; and when he was told he might look again, he saw she had tied the stocking to the line and was running it out like a cradle into the dead waste of the night.

"Hendry Watty! Hendry Watty! look out below!"

Before he could answer, plump! a man's leg came tumbling past his ear and scattered the ashes right and left.

"Hendry Watty! Hendry Watty! look out below!"

This time 'twas a great white arm and hand, with a silver ring sunk tight in the flesh of the little finger.

"Hendry Watty! Hendry Watty! warm them limbs!"

My grandfather picked them up and was warming them before the fire, when down came tumbling a great round head and bounced twice and lay in the firelight, staring up at him. And whose head was it but Archelaus Rowett's, that he'd run away from once already that night.

"Hendry Watty! Hendry Watty! look out below!"

This time 'twas another leg, and my grandfather was just about to lay hands on it, when the woman called down:

"Hendry Watty! catch it quick! It's my own leg I've thrown down by mistake."

The leg struck the ground and bounced high, and Hendry Watty made a leap after it.

And I reckon it's asleep he must have been; for what he caught was not Mrs. Rowett's leg, but the jib-boom of a deep-laden brigantine that was running him down in the dark. And as he sprang for it, his boat was crushed by the brigantine's fore-foot and went down under his very boot-soles. At the same time he let out a yell, and two or three of the crew ran forward and hoisted him up to the bowsprit and in on deck, safe and sound.

But the brigantine happened to be outward bound for the River Plate; so that, with one thing and another, 'twas eleven good months before my grandfather landed again at Port Loe. And who should be the first man he sees standing above the cove but William John Dunn.

"I'm very glad to see you," says William John Dunn.

"Thank you kindly," answers my grandfather; "and how's Mary Polly?"

"Why, as for that," he says, "she took so much looking after, that I couldn't feel I was properly keeping her under my eye till I married her, last June month."

"You was always one to over-do things," said my grandfather.

"But if you was alive an' well, why didn' you drop us a line?"

Now when it came to talk about "dropping a line," my grandfather fairly lost his temper. So he struck William John Dunn on the nose — a thing he had never been known to do before — and William John Dunn hit him back, and the neighbors had to separate them. And next day, William John Dunn took out a summons against him. Well, the case was tried before the magistrates: and my grandfather told his story from the beginning, quite straightforward, just as I've told it to you. And the magistrates decided that, taking one thing and another, he'd had a great deal of provocation, and fined him five shillings. And there the matter ended. But now you know the reason why I'm William John Dunn's grandson instead of Hendry Watty's.

CHILDE ROWLAND

Childe Rowland and his brothers twain

Were playing at the ball,

And there was their sister Burd Ellen

In the midst, among them all.

Childe Rowland kicked it with his foot

And caught it with his knee;

At last as he plunged among them all

O'er the church he made it flee.

Burd Ellen round about the aisle

To seek the ball is gone,

But long they waited, and longer still,

And she came not back again.

They sought her east, they sought her west,

They sought her up and down,

And woe were the hearts of those brethren,

For she was not to be found.

SO at last her eldest brother went to the Warlock Merlin and told him all the case, and asked him if he knew where Burd Ellen was. "The fair Burd Ellen," said the Warlock Merlin, "must have been carried off by the fairies, because she went round the church 'widershins'—the opposite way to the sun. She is now in the Dark Tower of the King of Elfland; it would take the boldest knight in Christendom to bring her back."

"If it is possible to bring her back," said her brother, "I'll do it, or perish in the attempt."

"Possible it is," said the Warlock Merlin, "but woe to the man or mother's son that attempts it, if he is not well taught beforehand what he is to do."

The eldest brother of Burd Ellen was not to be put off, by any fear of danger, from attempting to get her back, so he begged the Warlock Merlin to tell him what he should do, and what he should not do, in going to seek his sister. And after he had been taught, and had repeated his lesson, he set out for Elfland.

But long they waited, and longer still,

With doubt and muckle pain,

But woe were the hearts of his brethren,

For he came not back again.

Then the second brother got tired and tired of waiting, and he went to the Warlock Merlin and asked him the same as his brother. So he set out to find Burd Ellen.

But long they waited, and longer still,

With muckle doubt and pain,

And woe were his mother's and brother's heart,

For he came not back again.

And when they had waited and waited a good long time, Childe Rowland, the youngest of Burd Ellen's brothers, wished to go, and went to his mother, the good queen, to ask her to let him go. But she would not at first, for he was the last and dearest of her children, and if he was lost, all would be lost. But he begged, and he begged, till at last the good queen let him go, and gave him his father's good brand that never struck in vain, and as she girt it round his waist, she said the spell that would give it victory.

So Childe Rowland said good-by to the good queen, his mother, and went to the cave of the Warlock Merlin. "Once more, and but once more," he said to the Warlock, "tell how man or mother's son may rescue Burd Ellen and her brothers twain."

"Well, my son," said the Warlock Merlin, "there are but two things, simple they may seem, but hard they are to do. One thing to do, and one thing not to do. And the thing to do is this: after you have entered the land of Fairy,

144

whoever speaks to you, till you meet the Burd Ellen, you must out with your father's brand and off with their head. And what you've not to do is this: bite no bit, and drink no drop, however hungry or thirsty you be; drink a drop or bite a bit, while in Elfland you be and never will you see Middle Earth again."

So Childe Rowland said the two things over and over again, till he knew them by heart, and he thanked the Warlock Merlin and went on his way. And he went along, and along, and along, and still further along, till he came to the horse-herd of the King of Elfland feeding his horses. These he knew by their fiery eyes, and knew that he was at last in the land of Fairy. "Canst thou tell me," said Childe Rowland to the horse-herd, "where the King of Elfland's Dark Tower is?" "I cannot tell thee," said the horse-herd, "but go on a little further and thou wilt come to the cow-herd, and he, maybe, can tell thee."

Then, without a word more, Childe Rowland drew the good brand that never struck in vain, and off went the horse-herd's head, and Childe Rowland went on further, till he came to the cow-herd, and asked him the same question. "I can't tell thee," said he, "but go on a little further, and thou wilt come to the hen-wife, and she is sure to know." Then Childe Rowland out with his good brand, that never struck in vain, and off went the cow-herd's head. And he went on a little further, till he came to an old woman in a gray cloak, and he asked her if she knew where the Dark Tower of the King of Elfland was. "Go on a little further," said the hen-wife, "till you come to a round green hill, surrounded with terrace-rings, from the bottom to the top; go round it three times, 'widershins,' and each time say:

"'Open, door! open, door!

And let me come in,'

and the third time the door will open, and you may go in." And Childe Rowland was just going on, when he remembered what he had to do; so he out with the good brand, that never struck in vain, and off went the hen-wife's head.

Then he went on, and on, and on, till he came to the round green hill with the terrace-rings from top to bottom, and he went round it three times, "widershins," saying each time:

"Open, door! open, door!

And let me come in."

And the third time the door did open, and he went in, and it closed with a click, and Childe Rowland was left in the dark.

It was not exactly dark, but a kind of twilight or gloaming. There were neither windows nor candles, and he could not make out where the twilight came from, if not through the walls and roof. There were rough arches made of a transparent rock, incrusted with sheepsilver and rock spar, and other bright stones. But though it was rock, the air was quite warm, as it always is in Elfland. So he went through this passage till at last he came to two wide and high folding-doors which stood ajar. And when he opened them, there he saw a most wonderful and glorious sight. A large and spacious hall, so large that it seemed to be as long, and as broad, as the green hill itself. The roof was supported by fine pillars, so large and lofty, that the pillars of a cathedral were as nothing to them. They were all of gold and silver, with fretted work, and between them and around them wreaths of flowers, composed of what do you think? Why, of diamonds and emeralds, and all manner of precious stones. And the very key-stones of the arches had for ornaments clusters of diamonds and rubies, and pearls, and other precious stones. And all these arches met in the middle of the roof, and just there, hung by a gold chain, an immense lamp made out of one big pearl hollowed out and quite transparent. And in the middle of this was a big, huge carbuncle, which kept spinning round and round, and this was what gave light by its rays to the whole hall, which seemed as if the setting sun was shining on it.

The hall was furnished in a manner equally grand, and at one end of it was a glorious couch of velvet, silk and gold, and there sat Burd Ellen, combing her golden hair with a silver comb. And when she saw Childe Rowland she stood up and said:

"God pity ye, poor luckless fool,

What have ye here to do?

"Hear ye this, my youngest brother,

Why didn't ye bide at home?

Had you a hundred thousand lives

Ye couldn't spare any a one.

"But sit ye down; but woe, O, woe,

That ever ye were born,

For come the King of Elfland in,

Your fortune is forlorn."

Then they sat down together, and Childe Rowland told her all that he had done, and she told him how their two brothers had reached the Dark Tower, but had been enchanted by the King of Elfland, and lay there entombed as if dead. And then after they had talked a little longer Childe Rowland began to feel hungry from his long travels, and told his sister Burd Ellen how hungry he was and asked for some food, forgetting all about the Warlock Merlin's warning.

Burd Ellen looked at Childe Rowland sadly, and shook her head, but she was under a spell, and could not warn him. So she rose up, and went out, and soon brought back a golden basin full of bread and milk. Childe Rowland was just going to raise it to his lips, when he looked at his sister and remembered why he had come all that way. So he dashed the bowl to the ground, and said: "Not a sup will I swallow, nor a bit will I bite, till Burd Ellen is set free."

Just at that moment they heard the noise of some one approaching, and a loud voice was heard saying:

"Fee, fi, fo, fum,

I smell the blood of a Christian man,

Be he dead, be he living, with my brand,

147

I'll dash his brains from his brain-pan."

And then the folding-doors of the hall were burst open, and the King of Elfland rushed in.

"Strike, then, Bogle, if thou darest," shouted out Childe Rowland, and rushed to meet him with his good brand that never yet did fail. They fought, and they fought, and they fought, till Childe Rowland beat the King of Elfland down on to his knees, and caused him to yield and beg for mercy. "I grant thee mercy," said Childe Rowland; "release my sister from thy spells and raise my brothers to life, and let us all go free, and thou shalt be spared." "I agree," said the Elfin King, and rising up he went to a chest from which he took a phial filled with a blood-red liquor. With this he anointed the ears, eyelids, nostrils, lips, and finger-tips of the two brothers, and they sprang at once into life, and declared that their souls had been away, but had now returned. The Elfin King then said some words to Burd Ellen, and she was disenchanted, and they all four passed out of the hall, through the long passage, and turned their back on the Dark Tower, never to return again. So they reached home, and the good queen their mother and Burd Ellen never went round a church "widershins" again.

TAM O' SHANTER

IT was market-day in the town of Ayr in Scotland. The farmers had come into town from all the country round about, to sell or exchange their farm produce, and buy what they needed to take home.

Amongst these farmers was a man by the name of Tam o' Shanter; a good natured, happy-go-lucky sort of person, but, I am sorry to say, somewhat of a drunkard.

Now Tam's wife, whose name was Kate, was a grievous scold; always nagging and faultfinding, and I fear making it far easier for Tam to do wrong than if she had treated him more kindly. However that may be, Tam was happier away from home; and this day had escaped his wife's scolding tongue, mounted his good gray mare Meg, and galloped off as fast as he could go to Market.

Tam, who was bent upon having a spree, found his good friend, the shoemaker Johnny, and off they went to their favorite ale house; where they stayed telling stories and singing and drinking, till late at night.

At last the time came to go home and Tam who had forgotten the long miles between him and the farm set forth, but a terrible storm had risen; the wind blew, the rain fell in torrents and the thunder roared long and loud.

It was a fearful night, black as pitch except for the blinding flashes of lightning; but Tam was well mounted on his good gray mare Maggie, and splashed along through the wind and mire, holding on to his good blue bonnet, and singing aloud an old Scotch sonnet; while looking about him with prudent care lest the bogies catch him unawares.

At last he drew near to the old ruined church of Alloway. For many, many years this old church had been roofless, but the walls were standing and it still retained the bell.

For many years it was said that the ghosts and witches nightly held their revels there, and sometimes rang the old bell. As Tam was crossing the ford of the stream called the Doon, which flowed nearby, he looked up at

149

the old church on the hillside above him, and behold! it was all ablaze with lights, and sounds of mirth and dancing reached his ears.

Now Tam had been made fearless by old John Barleycorn, and he made good Maggie take him close to the church so that he could look inside, and there he saw the weirdest sight—

Witches and ghosts in a mad dance, and the music was furnished by the Devil himself in the shape of a beast, who played upon the bagpipes, and made them scream so loud that the very rafters rang with the sound.

It was an awful sight; and as Tam looked in, amazed and curious, the fun and mirth grew fast and furious.

The Piper loud and louder blew, and the dancers quick and quicker flew.

One of the witches resembled a handsome girl that Tam had known called Nannie; Tam sat as one bewitched watching her as she danced, and at last losing his wits altogether, called out: "Weel done, Cutty-Sark!"—and in an instant all was dark!

He had scarcely time to turn Maggie round, when all the legion of witches and spirits were about him like a swarm of angry bees. As a crowd runs, when the cry "Catch the thief" is heard, so runs Maggie; and the witches follow with many an awful screech and halloo! Hurry, Meg! Do thy utmost! Win the keystone of the bridge, for a running stream they dare not cross! Then you can toss your tail at them! But before good Meg could reach the keystone of the bridge she had no tail to toss. For Nannie far before the rest, hard upon noble Maggie prest, and flew at Tam with fury. But she little knew good Maggie's mettle. With one spring, she brought off her master safe, but left behind her own gray tail!

The witch had caught it and left poor Maggie with only a stump.

Tam O' Shanter

"Of brownys and of bogilis full is this buke."—Gawin Douglas.

When chapman billies leave the street,

And drouthy neebors neebors meet,

As market-days are wearing late,
An' folk begin to tak' the gate;
While we sit bousing at the nappy,
An' gettin' fou and unco happy,
We think na on the lang Scots miles,
The mosses, waters, slaps, and stiles,
That lie between us and our hame,
Where sits our sulky sullen dame,
Gathering her brows like gathering storm,
Nursing her wrath to keep it warm.
This truth fand honest Tam o' Shanter,
As he frae Ayr ae night did canter,
(Auld Ayr, wham ne'er a town surpasses,
For honest men and bonny lasses.)
O Tam! hadst thou but been sae wise,
As ta'en thy ain wife Kate's advise!
She tauld thee weel thou was a skellum,
A blethering, blustering, drunken blellum;
That frae November till October,
Ae market-day thou wasna sober;
That ilka melder, wi' the miller,
Thou sat as lang as thou had siller;
That ev'ry naig was ca'd a shoe on,
The smith and thee gat roaring fou on;
That at the Lord's house, ev'n on Sunday,
Thou drank wi' Kirton Jean till Monday.

She prophesy'd, that late or soon,
Thou would be found deep drown'd in Doon;
Or catch'd wi' warlocks in the mirk,
By Alloway's auld haunted kirk.
Ah, gentle dames! it gars me greet,
To think how mony counsels sweet,
How mony lengthen'd sage advices,
The husband frae the wife despises!
But to our tale: — Ae market night,
Tam had got planted unco right;
Fast by an ingle bleezing finely,
Wi' reaming swats, that drank divinely;
And at his elbow, Souter Johnny,
His ancient, trusty, drouthy crony;
Tam lo'ed him like a vera brither;
They had been fou' for weeks thegither!
The night drave on wi' sangs an' clatter;
And ay the ale was growing better:
The storm without might rair and rustle —
Tam did na mind the storm a whistle.
Care, made to see a man sae happy,
E'en drown'd himself amang the nappy!
As bees flee hame wi' lades o' treasure,
The minutes wing'd their way wi' pleasure:
Kings may be blest, but Tam was glorious,
O'er a' the ills o' life victorious.

But pleasures are like poppies spread,
You seize the flow'r, its bloom is shed;
Or like the snow falls in the river,
A moment white—then melts for ever;
Or like the borealis race,
That flit ere you can point their place;
Or like the rainbow's lovely form
Evanishing amid the storm.
Nae man can tether time or tide;
The hour approaches Tam maun ride;
That hour, o' night's black arch the kay-stane,
That dreary hour he mounts his beast in;
And sic a night he taks the road in
As ne'er poor sinner was abroad in.
The wind blew as 'twad blawn its last;
The rattling show'rs rose on the blast;
The speedy gleams the darkness swallow'd;
Loud, deep, and lang the thunder bellow'd:
That night, a child might understand,
The De'il had business on his hand.
Weel mounted on his gray mare, Meg,
A better never lifted leg,
Tam skelpit on thro' dub and mire,
Despising wind, and rain, and fire;
Whiles holding fast his guid blue bonnet;
Whiles crooning o'er some auld Scots sonnet;

Whiles glow'ring round wi' prudent cares,
Les bogles catch him unawares;
Kirk-Alloway was drawing nigh,
Where ghaists and houlets nightly cry.
By this time he was cross the foord,
Whare in the snaw the chapman smoor'd;
And past the birks and meikle stane,
Where drunken Charlie brak's neck-bane;
And thro' the whins, and by the cairn,
Where hunters fand the murder'd bairn;
And near the thorn, aboon the well,
Where Mungo's mither hang'd hersel'.
Before him Doon pours all his floods;
The doubling storm roars thro' the woods;
The lightnings flash from pole to pole;
Near and more near the thunders roll;
When, glimmering thro' the groaning trees,
Kirk-Alloway seem'd in a bleeze;
Thro' ilka bore the beams were glancing;
And loud resounded mirth and dancing.
Inspiring, bold John Barleycorn!
What dangers thou canst make us scorn!
Wi' tippenny, we fear nae evil;
Wi' usquabae we'll face the devil!
The swats sae ream'd in Tammie's noodle,
Fair play, he car'd nae deils a boddle.

But Maggie stood right sair astonish'd,
'Till, by the heel and hand admonish'd,
She ventur'd forward on the light;
And wow! Tam saw an unco sight!
Warlocks and witches in a dance;
Nae cotillion brent new frae France,
But hornpipes, jigs, strathspeys, and reels,
Put life and mettle in their heels:
A winnock-bunker in the east,
There sat auld Nick, in shape o' beast;
A towzie tyke, black, grim, and large,
To gie them music was his charge;
He screw'd the pipes and gart them skirl,
Till roof and rafters a' did dirl— As
Tammie glowr'd, amaz'd, and curious,
The mirth and fun grew fast and furious:
The piper loud and louder blew;
The dancers quick and quicker flew;
They reel'd, they set, they cross'd, they cleekit,
'Til ilka carlin swat and reekit,
And coost her duddies to the wark,
And linket at it in her sark!
But Tam kenn'd what was what fu' brawlie,
There was a winsome wench and walie,
That night enlisted in the core,
(Lang after kenn'd on Carrick shore;

For mony a beast to dead she shot,
And perish'd mony a bonnie boat,
And shook baith meikle corn and bear,
And kept the country-side in fear.)
Her cutty sark, o' Paisley harn,
That, while a lassie, she had worn,
In longitude tho' sorely scanty,
It was her best, and she was vauntie.
Ah! little kenn'd thy reverend grannie,
That sark she coft for her wee Nannie,
Wi' twa pund Scots ('twas a' her riches),
Wad ever grac'd a dance of witches!
But here my muse her wing maun cour;
Sic flights are far beyond her pow'r;
To sing how Nannie lap and flang,
(A soup'e jade she was and strang),
And how Tam stood, like ane bewitch'd,
And thought his very een enrich'd;
Even Satan glowr'd, and fidg'd fu' fain,
And hotch'd and blew wi' might and main:
'Til first ae caper, syne anither,
Tam tint his reason a' thegither,
And roars out, "Well done, Cutty-sark!"
And in an instant all was dark:
And scarcely had he Maggie rallied,
When out the hellish legion sallied.

As bees bizz out wi' angry gyke,
When plundering herds assail their byke;
As open pussie's mortal foes,
When, pop! she starts before their nose;
As eager runs the market-crowd,
When "Catch the thief!" resounds aloud;
So Maggie runs, the witches follow,
Wi' mony an eldritch screech and hollow.
Ah, Tam! Ah, Tam! thou'll get thy fairin'!
In hell they'll roast thee like a herrin'!
In vain thy Kate awaits thy comin'!
Kate soon will be a woefu' woman!
Now do thy speedy utmost, Meg,
And win the key-stane of the brig;
There at them thou thy tail may toss,
A running stream they darena cross!
But ere the key-stane she could make,
The fient a tail she had to shake!
For Nannie, far before the rest,
Hard upon noble Maggie prest,
And flew at Tammie wi' furious ettle;
But little wist she Maggie's mettle—
Ae spring brought off her master hale,
But left behind her ain gray tail:
The carlin claught her by the rump,
And left poor Maggie scarce a stump.

Now, wha this tale o' truth shall read,
Ilk man and mother's son, take heed:
Whene'er to drink you are inclin'd,
Or cutty-sarks run in your mind,
Think! ye may buy the joys o'er dear —
Remember Tam o' Shanter's mare.
ROBERT BURNS.

THE BOGGART

IN an old farm-house in Yorkshire, where lived an honest farmer named George Gilbertson, a Boggart had taken up his abode. He caused a good deal of trouble, and he kept tormenting the children, day and night, in various ways. Sometimes their bread and butter would be snatched away, or their porringers of bread and milk be capsized by an invisible hand; for the Boggart never let himself be seen; at other times the curtains of their beds would be shaken backwards and forwards, or a heavy weight would press on and nearly suffocate them. Their mother had often, on hearing their cries, to fly to their aid.

There was a kind of closet, formed by a wooden partition on the kitchen-stairs, and a large knot having been driven out of one of the deal-boards of which it was made, there remained a round hole. Into this, one day, the farmer's youngest boy stuck the shoe-horn with which he was amusing himself, when immediately it was thrown out again, and struck the boy on the head. Of course it was the Boggart did this, and it soon became their sport, which they called larking with the Boggart, to put the shoe-horn into the hole and have it shot back at them. But the gamesome Boggart at length proved such a torment that the farmer and his wife resolved to quit the house and let him have it all to himself. This settled, the flitting day came, and the farmer and his family were following the last loads of furniture, when a neighbor named John Marshall came up.

"Well, Georgey," said he, "and so you're leaving t'ould hoose at last?"

"Heigh, Johnny, my lad, I'm forced to it; for that bad Boggart torments us so, we can neither rest night nor day for't. It seems to have such a malice against t'poor bairns, it almost kills my poor dame here at thoughts on't, and so, ye see, we're forced to flitt loike."

He scarce had uttered the words when a voice from a deep upright churn cried out. "Aye, aye, Georgey, we're flittin ye see!"

"Ods, alive!" cried the farmer, "if I'd known thou would flit too, I'd not have stirred a peg!"

And with that, he turned about to his wife, and told her they might as well stay in the old house, as be bothered by the Boggart in a new one. So stay they did.

THE END

Milton Keynes UK
Ingram Content Group UK Ltd.
UKHW040749181023
430769UK00004B/148